CU01025111

Knife Song Korea

œ

excelsior editions

AN IMPRINT OF STATE UNIVERSITY OF NEW YORK PRESS

Knife Song Korea

A NOVEL

Richard Selzer

Published by
STATE UNIVERSITY OF NEW YORK PRESS, ALBANY

For information, contact State University of New York Press, Albany, NY
www.sunypress.edu

Production and book design, Laurie Searl
Marketing, Fran Keneston

Library of Congress Cataloging-in-Publication Data

Selzer, Richard,
1928–
Knife song Korea : a novel / Richard Selzer.
p. cm.
ISBN 978-1-4384-2761-4 (alk. paper)
I. Title.
PS3569.E585K56 2009
813'.54—dc22
2008055625

10   9   8   7   6   5   4   3   2   1

PART I

Land of the Morning Calm

chapter one

He kept his head bowed all the way up the steep path. It was April and the Korean hillsides, having persevered all winter, complaining under the snow, were suddenly extravagant with pink jindala that broke out on their thick brown hides like a rash. It was cold as he neared the summit. He drew into himself, less of a target to the wind. The ground was flat where he stood on a small plateau. On one side he could see the vast valley from which he had mounted, on the other he looked down upon the Yellow Sea. A misnomer, he thought, it's the Gray Sea, gray as a timberwolf and rabid, lying on its side, flanks heaving with forced respiration and the spume of the waves like spittle bubbling from its jaws.

Someone had carved a great stone Buddha on the summit. Sloane walked to it, leaned against the granite pedestal and lit a cigarette. *Until the East Sea's waves are dry* went "Augukka," the Korean national anthem, but the Buddha gazed out over the sea with an expression of nausea, as though even the sight of that ocean made him seasick. The faint grimace, the lowered lids, seemed to be a suppression of gastric distress. Like me, Sloane thought.

Korea. With his entry into this country he had begun the ordeal that would lead him to his manhood, or death—or both. Everything that had gone before—his decision to be a doctor, medical school, surgical training—had taken place in a kind of nursery. He had been called Doctor there, had gotten married, performed operations, delivered babies, but he had only been dressed in his father's clothes *playing* grownup, *playing* doctor.

"Why do you want to be a doctor?" the chairman of the admissions committee had asked him.

Sloane had looked at the center of his polkadot tie, the little knot like the head of a kingpin in the man's neck which, if pulled, would cause that crew-cut, razor-lipped, small-eyed head to roll across the table like the yield of a guillotine. Who would wear such a tie at a time like this? Or such a ridiculous white mustache, pencil thin? With a straight face he had said, "I find the material interesting." He had calculated it well in advance, knowing they would be looking for the slightest sign of frailty, softness, pity. He wouldn't be caught there. Nor could he have told the simple truth. "To swim in the very stream, sir, not walk alongside of it." No, he knew who they wanted him to be. Pure objective. Man of science. No faggotry. Be crisp and let them see you in a laboratory titrating body fluids, *not* holding a hand, helping mankind, anchoring a heart to courage. No wit either. Risk being a bit of a bore. "I find the material interesting." And he was accepted.

He had crossed the water on a troop transport along with twelve other doctors and the backbone of Medical Company 102 of the Seventh Division Artillery. From Japan it was eastward until there was no more east. They had docked at midnight, were unloaded at Pusan by three in the morning. It was January and cold in the darkness of an anemic moon with flashlights curtly waving them on to a comfortless beginning. Loaded into the open back of a two-ton truck with thirty others of his kind, he was treated to his first Korean roads, so pitted and rutted as to be felt in every cell. Pressed close together, the men in the truck did not huddle for warmth, they did not even talk. It was a sober enactment of anxiety and the need not to show it. The intermittent flare of cigarettes made the truck seem infested with phosphorescent bugs. Now and then one of these insects would arc from the truck in an apparent suicide. Easily understandable. By morning they were ensconced in an abandoned Japanese jail. Three to a cell plus rats made a crowd. Men and beasts crouched and eyed each other yellowly in the glare of a naked bulb. Sloane fell into a damp and restless sleep. They parted the next morning.

The trip north was in the noisiest conveyance he had known, wheezing and coughing as if it had contracted emphysema from the dust. Sloane saw that the driver had at least two talents: driving through potholes and spitting. Each time they were catapulted, doll-like, the driver would shake his head, lean out of the jeep and propel a dollop of spittle into the cloud of brown and putrid dust. It had become twilight and still they headed north. Sloane slouched in his seat, willing limpness into his body, giving himself up to the battering. He discovered that if he rested his elbows on his knees and let his bowed head swing forward freely between the shoulders, he could avoid the headache that came stronger and stronger with each transmission up the spinal column. He was certain that with each blow a tiny punctate hemorrhage appeared in his brain. He felt his cerebration dulling. If the trip were long enough he would lumber from the jeep slope-browed and forever stupid.

Korea. The name reminded him of a disease, chorea, characterized by aimless jerky movements of the body: St. Vitus Dance. It was fitting. Since he felt no purpose here, his arms and his legs had no purpose either. With the decision not to resist came a measure of relief, small to be sure, but enough to make thought again possible. He felt schizophrenic, as though he were watching himself from elsewhere, but the alienation gave a patina of numbness to his discomfort, like receiving a shot of morphine. The pain was still there but one no longer cared.

Between jolts, pictures of his life slipped into view like lantern slides. He rejected each one until he saw himself at 8 o'clock filing with the other white coats into the cold amphitheater for Grand Rounds. From this distance they looked like prisoners in a concentration camp forced to watch an execution. The crime: surfeit of life—inadvertent misuse of the body. For a moment the picture stuck and they were no more than gravestones on a hill. Last to arrive was the bed bearing the patient, abandoned in despair in the presentation pit at the center of the hall. Her black head protruded from the covers, an old cracked boot, tongue unslung and flipping over the side.

"Jessie Atkins is a sixty-eight-year-old widowed Negro female," the intern intoned, "who was admitted to the hospital ten days ago with the complaint of having fallen unconscious on the street."

A hard jolt threw him bruisingly against the door. The driver swore softly and ground the gears. Sloane turned to the side and settled himself in the seat, his body seeking a comfort that was not there. With each hour of buffeting, Sloane's fear increased. It seemed incredible that he would ever return through this place. Were there in fact people at the end of this journey, people who expected him? Would there be edible food, clean water, conversation? Or—if it ever ended, if there were a destination—would it be a hillside, one of these many, with only himself to guard it or whatever the army made men do with hillsides? He wanted a drink, an old-fashioned, then he wanted to fly home. He closed his eyes. He would think of cool woods, blue skies, foxes and pheasants.

文

"There it is, sir, Seven Div Arty," said Gallagher, the driver, and the jeep, coughing, rolled to a halt.

If I open my eyes, Sloane thought, I am committed, it will be real. If I keep them closed . . .

What he saw was a brown hillside dotted by darker brown tents in rows, a few brown Quonset huts like the shucked skins of giant slugs, and a flat bulldozed place for trucks, ambulances, jeeps.

"Give it to me straight," Sloane said to the medical officer who had opened the door of the jeep and was accompanying him to a cave-shaped tent with a central stove and planked floor, the jamesway that would be his home.

"Really? Straight, eh?"

His name was Larry Olsen, a doctor from New Jersey.

"B.S. won't help me."

"No, it will not. Well then, it's simple: you're my replacement."

"How many of us are there?"

"Just you. You are *the* replacement. No bullshit? It's bad. Bad, boring, degrading. The fucking war came through here six months ago. We took a lot of casualties. Bloody scene for a while. It broke the monotony. But the war moved on. We didn't. You won't. You're assigned to all the villages in the province. All of them. There's no duty like it. There's nothing *in this world* like it. You work through interpreters. There's no roof that doesn't leak. The rats are fearless. Flies rule the country. Everybody steals. Orphans, refugees everywhere. They're coming down from the north. There's no equipment to speak of. There's no sterilizer. And the dirt, the vermin. I just plain don't touch *anybody* unless I have to— *had* to—*had* to. It's *yours* now. I'm sorry about that but I've been waiting for you forever. You said you wanted it straight. *You'll* be waiting for *your* replacement forever. That'll start today. It's better than fighting in the field, force-feeding on C rations and freezing to death, but . . . that does *not* change the fact that morale is impossible, so don't even look for it and don't look for home, either. Where're you from?"

"I was up at Yale."

"Yeah, well, listen to me: New Haven, New Jersey, New York, Philly, Boston, D.C., the White House, the Grand

Fucking Canyon—none of those places exist or *ever* existed here. You will see them wiped out by the day. Now I'm going to get it all back. *I'll* do the erasing. If I never hear the word Korea, if there *is* no Korea, that'll be okay. "

Sloane looked at him. Gleaming belt buckle decorating a paunch. Shiny boots, blue eyes, and meaning what he said.

"When are you leaving?"

"Tomorrow morning."

"Tomorrow?"

"*To*-morrow."

"That's not possible."

"Look, Sloane—I wish with all my heart that I could take you with me. I don't have to know you to know that you don't deserve it—none of us deserves it. We're physicians, but not for this. But we're in the army now, so—"

"But how can you be leaving tomorrow?"

"Let me put it to you this way. If, by some ill wind—a storm, a shift in the war—I were detained for a few days, you'd be looking at a bullet in my brain, conducting the autopsy. *One* more night, *one* more morning—that's about all is left in me."

"How am I to know what to do?"

"You'll be fine about that. The Korean boys'll show you the routine. They're a pair all right but they're the best. Keep them alive, keep 'em close to you, you won't slide in too deep if you can help it."

Olsen excused himself. Clearly his time now was budgeted. He was as short as it gets.

Sloane returned to Gallagher the spitter, a heavy-set Carolinian whose job it was to repair the ambulance and jeep after each convulsive trip.

"Gallagher—what's the routine here?"

Gallagher climbed around in the engine with a wrench and a large pair of pliers as he spoke. With youthful agility he shifted his stocky frame and his head would disappear into the works and reemerge with a black smear on his face or his ungloved hands.

"Better ask Jang, sir. He runs the shootin match. Far as *I* know it's G.I. sick call mornin, local the afternoon, whatever else pops up along the way."

"Like what?"

"Babies. Pendicitis. Splosions. Fucking fields—sorry, sir—fields are *full* of land mines. Every time a papa-san walks his ox and his fucking plow—walks his plow down a field, sir, he's takin a big chance. Lot of em here without a leg, big holes in'er guts. Ought to see them fucking cows—*that's* a blast."

"Jang runs the show?"

"Yup, him and Yoon. They're good at it, Doc. You won't have to do much, only the big stuff. Them two katusas are as good as any stateside doctor I ever met."

"Living is *not* what I do best," he had said to Kate, the orders sending him to Korea in his hand just five months after they had been married. "Look at my destination: Sasebo. An airfield near Yokohama, but it sounds like something growing on your nose."

She had hidden her feelings if she had had any. Her face was like a pond after a frog has jumped in it, a pond that tidies up the ripples, muffles the sound, hastens back into the quiet reflection that is most becoming. She was beautiful to him and she was resourceful. She could live quite well and courageously without him, he was certain of this. When he was boarding the plane she slid her fingers beneath his lapels and rubbed with her thumbs the little brass caduceus in each. He had said that he wanted no goodbyes. He looked for but could not find a higher shine to the eyes, a tight little pallor around the lips, the whisk of a tremor across the cheek.

"Do whatever is appropriate," she said very softly. "Now, and later."

It had made perfect sense when she said it. Now it worried him. Did she mean that she, too, would do "whatever is appropriate," and if so, what would that entail? He was annoyed with himself for not having asked her exactly what she meant. Now it was too late to ask because it was too late, probably, to know.

Sloane rose early after a restless night. He was anxious to see what it looked like in daylight. Surely there must be some charm to it. He stepped to the door of the jamesway and threw it open. It had snowed heavily during the night and the post had taken on the desolation of a Russian army barracks. The great bulk of things—tents, vehicles, Quonset huts—were submerged under many feet of snow and what protruded was a tiny portion of each, giving the impression that all of life transpired under the snow in a labyrinth of passages and cubicles.

When he stepped out into the cool air, two Koreans squatting on their haunches, dressed in the drab winter fatigues of the army, were worrying a dying rat with a stick. As he watched, one reached out and poked the beast on its snout. It reacted by baring its yellowish fangs and whipping its head in their direction as though to attack. After a few seconds of bristling and reflex rage, the rat sank onto its side and resumed the labored breathing. It suffered silently, the eyes staring along the snow, unseeing, uncaring. The other Korean took his turn with the stick, sliding it beneath the upper trunk and flipping the rat into the air. He screamed with laughter as the rat fell back to earth near their feet. It lay still for a time, then rose unsteadily and began to convulse. After a high sharp scream that weakened into a few staccato notes, they poked it without response. One of the Koreans stood up and prodded the carcass with his foot. They stood looking down at it, fascinated, a thrill quite visible on their faces. Sloane was slightly nauseated.

"What are you doing? Get out of here."

They had not seen him and were shocked by his outburst. They stood as one and saluted smartly. They looked like teenagers. He automatically returned their salute, feeling sheepish.

"Who are you?"

"I Jang, sir."

"I Yoon, sir."

They were both giggling like schoolgirls, as though the sound of their names was too ridiculous for words.

"What's so funny?"

They looked at each other, shook their heads and covered their mouths with cupped palms as though to hold in the laughing.

"We do rat patrol," said Jang. "See?"

He pointed to a wheelbarrow: a pile of dead rats lying heaped as they had been flung, eye to tail, white bellies crossed by tiny feet, snouts poking between adjacent bodies.

"Rat patrol?"

"Every morning, sir, rats die. Poison all round tents. Rats come night, eat. Morning die. See?"

They both laughed again, covering their mouths tightly. Sloane looked at the neighboring jamesways. Here and there lay the corpses of other rats, awaiting the patrol.

"Where do they put the poison?"

"Here. See poison?"

Sloane followed them to the corner of the jamesway. There was a pan covered with a wire net in which a handful of meal had been strewn.

"I see."

They were both the same height, short and slender. Each of their shirts bore a white strip above the pocket that gave his name and the letters ROKA: Army of the Republic of Korea.

"We katusa," said Yoon agreeably. "Korean. Attached to. United States Army."

"We help you. We your boys. You want something?"

"No, I don't want anything."

He made as if to reenter the jamesway. They followed him to the door.

"We crean tent, sir."

"Is that part of your job?"

"We your boys. We take care of you."

"I Jang."

"I Yoon."

They laughed heartily. He watched them fill a pan with water from a five-gallon can and set it on the pot-bellied stove.

"What's that for?"

"You wash and shave," said Yoon, motioning. Reaching into a carton, he drew out a white toilet seat and leaned it against the stove.

"What's that for?"

"You go john—three-holer." Yoon pointed up the hillside toward the outhouse. "You takee from stove. Sidown, nice'n warm. Everybody else sit on ice. Sir Doc nice'n warm. Be happy, see?"

"Looks as if I'm going to rot first class," Sloane said.

They burst into laughter as though they had understood.

"We medics, too," said Jang. "Go every prace you, all time we go you."

"How old are you?"

"I thirty."

Sloane was shocked.

"And you?"

"I twenty-eight."

He was glad they were older. It made him feel less threatened by their youth. They looked sixteen. Smooth chins, faces unlined. At the backs of their necks the twin columns of musculature, deeply cleft in the middle, were irregularly sprinkled with unruly boyish hair. But there was strength in their brown arms and rocky fists. There was nothing soft in their bodies, only when the eyelids lost their turgor and the eyes looked dreamily off and away. They did not talk about themselves, but later Yoon told him that Jang was from the north and had a wife up there. He had not seen her in two years. Jang said of Yoon: "We number one good buddy. Only sometimes"—and he shook his head disapprovingly—"he drink too much makju, go crazy." He drew a circle around his ear with his finger.

As Sloane shaved he could hear the rhythmic scraping of snow shovels. When he hitched through blizzards to Albany Medical College there was much to complain about but he refused to complain, for this was part of the adventure he had charted for himself: he was going to be a doctor. Not a doctor *easily*—a doctor, whatever it took. And he was a doctor *to practice*—wherever he might be. He reminded himself that what was true for Larry Olsen did not have to be true for him. Probably it was, but he would see about that.

chapter two

He paused in front of the large Quonset hut that was the dispensary and tried to evoke a positive response. It seemed to him an unlikely place to treat the sick. There is no building on earth uglier than this, he thought. It would be impossible to think of it as home or to feel a loyalty to it, the kind of devotion to brick and beam one feels upon returning to the place of an old struggle, joy, or sorrow, where even the weeds poking between stones are homely but dear. It was a single curved sheet of corrugated brown metal comprising at once roof and walls in one characterless sweep. Along the sides were small rectangles that must, he thought, be windows, although from the outside no translucency was apparent. Screening had been tacked across these apertures with khaki shades beneath, giving the structure a hooded air like those drawings of death from beneath whose deep cowl the most penetrating peer could evoke no physiognomy. The ends were sealed by sheets of the same corrugated metal in which doorways, a front and a back, had been cut. It was not sinister but had rather the blind, bloated, indifferent look of a swollen slug. It was a building without history: fungoid, charmless, beneath whose sweep events took place, no doubt, but failed to rouse in the viewer one jot of curiosity. Nothing grand or even wicked could happen herein. It had not even the sunken nobility of a tenement shack.

Sloane walked around it twice, looking for some small but telling detail—about what it didn't matter, for he was only looking to reinforce, at least, a sense of his own skill at observation, something to give him a little courage. But the hut told nothing. Of course not—that was the point of it. No way to gain an edge. There was a generator that did not appear to function but what that told him he did not want to hear.

Sloane took a deep breath, exhaled loudly, as if he were talking to himself, and stepped inside.

"A ten hut!"

The sharply barked order startled him visibly. He was certain his frightened jump had been seen by every man who leaped to his feet and now stood absurdly rigid. He had forgotten he was to be the commanding officer of a medical company. He looked in awe at the forest of sprung soldiers that vibrated, waiting for the *ease* which he forgot to tell them to be *at*.

They're *boys*, thought Sloane with expanding gloom.

"At ease."

It slid shyly from his lips. It was an awkward, embarrassed beginning.

"How do you do?" he said.

Oh my God. He could hear them at dinner that night, how-do-you-doing all over the mess hall. He was certain it was the first *how do you do* of the Korean War.

He read the nearest name tag.

"Corporal Johnson. I'm Lieutenant Sloane. Please show me the dispensary."

"Yes, sir. Follow me, sir."

As a medical facility it was surprisingly adequate. Moveable white partitions blocked off areas of the Quonset hut into a receiving space up front, four cubicles for examination, two treatment rooms, and an infirmary at the rear where eight cots were set up, four on each side of a central aisle.

"Is this all?"

"Yes, sir."

"No other buildings?"

"Not for us, sir. Vehicles down at the motor pool, sir. That's Gallagher. Would you like to see them?"

"No, not now. What's the schedule here?"

"Mostly G.I. sick call in the morning, sir, then we try to start the Koreans in the early afternoon."

"What do you mean *try to start* them?"

"A lot of emergencies any time, sir. There's not another facility like this one, sir, with a real doctor like you, sir, for probably fifty miles. That takes in a lot."

This was more or less what Gallagher and Larry Olsen had told him, only it seemed a lot more real to him now.

"What's the procedure for more equipment?"

"Well, sir, if I can tell you the truth, sir: you place an order, then you place the order again, then you place the order again and the equipment don't come. We ask help from some of the brass and they say something like, ah, well, 'We shall emphasize the urgency,' but that don't cut it, sir. Sorry, sir. We kinda figured out how to use what we have."

The rat patrol arrived. It was apparent that the others had been waiting for them to take charge.

"Sir Doc," they chorused, saluting. "Runch time. Go officers crub. Eat runch. Come back after, Korean sick call. Okay, Sir Doc?"

Sloane nodded and turned toward the door and tardily returned the flock of salutes that flew to twenty rigid brows. Outside the hut he lit a cigarette. How about an order for a drink, Sloane thought. Can you get that filled? On the way to the officers' mess his determination melted swiftly out of him and into the dirty snow. He hoped that he would be stricken by some dreadful disease requiring his prompt evacuation.

16

chapter three

Dearest Kate,
I don't think I like Korea. Can you come get me? I'm afraid
I got on the wrong bus tour.

Sloane's gaze drifted from the paper to the small window
in the jamesway. He looked out across the valley at the
mountains beyond. He had been trying to see Connecticut.

It is called the Land of the Morning Calm. I don't know why,
but in some curious way it fits the early morning, which is
wrapped in a stillness that is at once smoky and viscid. Up here
on this hill I can look down across the long winding valley, ter-
raced, green, dotted with mushroom-like huts—the thatch gives
them that effect. But nighttime is not calm at all, not for me,
which is why I am writing to you at midnight, my darling. And at
no time of day do I ever feel a part of this country. Unless it's the
fear of it closing over me, leaving no trace of my trespass.
I wish I knew you better.
Kate, you keep secrets.
That in itself is one of your secrets.
Here is one of mine:
You know that the flight to Fort Sam Houston was my first
flight ever. What you don't know is what I thought up there, near

the moon. *Of course I thought of you—I am always busting wide open with desire—every inch of me is crawling with the want of you, of course—but I thought this too: we're flying over alligators. I pictured them bellying the mud of Georgian swamps, poised among vines of great wickedness, their omnivorous mouths raised and held open in a stance of tireless greed. And with a little rush of fear I picked up my feet and tucked them under me, lest we swoop overlow and indiscreet. I should not wish to hear even the echo of those chops slapping shut in slow reptilian rage. It would stay with me a lifetime and I would grow slowly more hysterical, convinced of pigmented teethmarks all around my ankles, like the stigmata of some bestial crucifixion.*

It must be apparent by now that I am deep in my cups while this is being written. It feels like a flop, but I have no intention of rereading it. So, Wifelet, you must take it or leave it. But don't leave me. If you ever stop loving me I won't take you anyplace nice ever again.

Sloane marveled at how imaginary Kate had become to him and in so short a time. He pictured her less to enjoy the sight of her than to prove her existence. He was surprised at how vague and unconvincing she was. As a husband, a new and loving one, one who writes to her as Only Little One and Dearest Thing I Have, shouldn't he be doing better than that? This particular problem, he realized, was not mentioned in the lectures on *Psychological Warfare, Maintenance of Equipment,* or *Duty Roster and Punishment Book.* If only he had known, he'd have raised his hand and asked the bombastic captain from Mississippi what a soldier ought to do in order to keep his wife alive in a place like this.

chapter four

Sloane watched the boys running the VD clinic. It seemed to him a marvel of efficiency. The soldiers filed in front of Jang and sat on a stool. As each one took out his penis and milked the drops of thick creamy white pus, Jang wiped a glass slide across it and handed it to Yoon, who flamed it and set it on a rack to dry. As soon as the slides were ready, Yoon stained them with methylene blue and swept them under the microscope. The whole thing took less than five minutes per patient. The positives were grouped together outside the dispensary where they lay down, smoked, and chatted without the slightest show of embarrassment. Sloane thought he could even detect an air of pride in the afflicted group, a kind of swagger. When the whole line had passed through, Jang made a face of disgust at Yoon and they both shook their heads and laughed.

"What now?"

"Penishillin, Sir Doc."

They wheeled a cart loaded with vials of liquid penicillin, syringes, needles, alcohol, and cotton balls. The door at the end of the dispensary was open and Jang presented himself, calling out, "Okay you number ten fucking G.I. come on." As each one filed by, he undid his belt and slid his pants down, holding them at half-mast with one hand, his back to Yoon and Jang. As the buttocks were swabbed twice with an alcohol sponge and the needle sunk home, the complaints were vitriolic, each with its own musicality. "Ow you *sonofabitch fucking* bastard wait till I *get* you I *Jesus Christ* what'd you *use* a fucking *screw*driver?"

"Go back, mama-san. See you tomorrow."

文

Sloane read the memo on his desk. Headquarters said there were six thousand prostitutes in the province and six thousand troops. That's one for each, he thought, except there's one guy with two because *I* don't have one. Morning sick call takes care of that. The line of soldiers with gonorrhea extended out the back door of the dispensary and fifty feet into the parking lot where the last few, no longer protecting their place in line, spread out like the tuft at the end of a tail. Sloane never saw a Korean in the VD line.

Actually, he thought, gonorrhea is a peaceful, loving disease. I have no quarrel with it. In fact there's something rather sweet about it. When bombs are falling and grenades are being thrown, the body is in the business of burrowing, ducking, scurrying. The minute the sulfur drifts away and the bleeding stops, what does a man do? He straightens up, brushes himself off with a few peremptory pats, and casts his eye about for the nearest woman. With six thousand of them crawling out of the neighboring crannies, he doesn't have far to lope. Screw today, drip tomorrow.

The lovely thing about gonorrhea is microscopic, he thought. I wonder whether Jang and Yoon have noticed that? Reduced to its cellular structure it takes on a spectacular beauty, all stained glass and Persian carpets, shadings and meltings away, subtle shapes interlocking, unfolding, receding into dimness, then recurring boldly at just the right moment. Sheets of cells, clusters, rosettes, cobbled multicolored pavements, villages roofed in hued thatch or shingle iridescent, tiny blue beasts paired, herding, or on some lonely errand—all of this from sheathes rancid with yesterday's lovemaking. A man holds his injured penis gently, the boy-mouth curls in self-disgust while the fingers that lately gripped a gun and squeezed out streams of bullets are grown suddenly tender, sad and pitying, lifting the sickness up and out, resting it on the burry palm. Were he to weep it would be now when the sweet bird of his youth lies moist of beak, wizening of wing. Jang and Yoon, who saw so much of it during the day—did they dream of it at night, rivers of off-white pus forming in the mountains, running down and flooding their countryside with people slipping and sliding and drowning in it?

That night it rained a light rain and he started by thinking about his honeymoon with Kate, a time that was all rain and all pleasure, the deepest he had known, pleasure they couldn't capture on the Leica—black and silver, so precisely tooled and so expensive—that her father had given them, a camera they were too busy to take out of its case. But thoughts of his honeymoon led him, indirectly, to the six thousand prostitutes. Not all of them, only the six-thousandth. He wondered what exactly Six Thousand was doing then, and he wondered what she looked like, what she would be wearing or not, what shade of lipstick, and why she hadn't tried a little harder to find her match in the U.S. Army.

chapter five

The crowded dispensary was shockingly quiet, as though a plague had passed through. The grass around the Quonset hut had been trampled dry. The first downpour would transform it into mud. It was as though even the ground served to isolate this place from healthy humanity, a discouraging quarantine. The walls, despite a weekly scrubdown with creosote, seemed to spawn solid banks of microbes: bacteria, parasites, fungi. The metal and wood were by now laid across a lattice of cocci and bacilli that on hot still days could be seen to undulate. If the walls were to be scrubbed with penicillin, the entire structure would collapse.

Indecisive gusty winds tore through the valley, dipping between the mountains as through a wind tunnel. Bernouilli's Principle, Sloane thought on the way to the three-holer, hugging himself miserably. Always picks up speed in the narrows. It was still too early for bathing. The streams were painfully cold. The Koreans' last wash was in October. The air in the dispensary that morning was palpable witness to the long filthy winter without a single change of clothing.

At least one hundred Koreans were gathered around the dispensary. The line stretched down the hillside to the gatepost and beyond where perhaps another hundred clustered on the road. Sloane sat at his desk, dreading the start of sick call, loathing the filthy bodies, the feel of grimy skin, the mixed smell of kimchi and feces. "I just plain don't touch *anybody* unless I have to," Olsen had said. Sloane could see why. He dreaded the presence of disease all around him, the pus on his fingers, and everywhere the flies, damned flies who, as Olsen had said, rule the world, weaving an invisible net of disease around the whole body of us. Already now, as if to hurry along the advent of spring, they were settled, green-gold, to their feast, rubbing their legs voluptuously, pollinating lungs with the tuberculosis of strangers. *There's a way to wage war.* He pictured two opposing armies exchanging mouthfuls of heavy-laden breath, humid from their innermost recesses. Well: the very food from the ground is rich with the discharges of others. War . . .

For a moment he thought of Peter Brueghel, how his people would be scampering, flirting, eating while surrounded with animal life, and how for him that was animal life of another kind. He had always wondered how many of Brueghel's people were alive two years after they'd been painted. One plague would have wiped out all those ugly creatures. But then, what's the difference whether they die today or on Valentine's Day? The matter with me is too much refinement, he thought. These Koreans with their dirt and their smell are like bacteria growing on a plate of agar— and they are more alive than I am. *Altogether* too refined—I can't help myself, and yet I've got to shuck it, say what the hell, and plunge into it.

He stepped to the doorway and looked over the heads of the crowd at the long lines advancing.

"No more," he called to the soldier waving them on. Most of them were standing slightly bowed, looking at him out of the tops of their eyes. Children were strapped to their backs, scabby little heads thick with impetigo and cradle cap, lolling behind the mask-like downcast faces of the mothers.

"Koshikake dozo," he called out. "Sit down."

He had memorized a few commands in Japanese. Korean was too hard to pronounce, and often, despite his best efforts, they were unable to decipher his meaning. After thirty-five years of occupation and brainwashing there was hardly a Korean who didn't know Japanese, although no one would admit to it or use it openly. *If you speak about the tiger it will come* was a Korean proverb. Yes, especially if you speak in its own tongue. What must they have done, the Japanese, to warrant this national hatred? Was it the occupation alone? What am I talking about, he thought, *the occupation alone*—as if that shouldn't have been enough.

Despite the collective shame they all felt at his words, they settled to their haunches, a great undulating blanket about him. They looked like a patch of eggplant, the sun striking purple from their black hair.

Sloane hated the sense of the Great White Father towering above his lowly subjects and he hated the insidious way it bonded them together. But there it was: they were his patients. Sick call? For him it was all of Korea. A strange enough fate. He certainly didn't predict it, neither did Kate—who was being awfully good about it. So far. And where, now, was his predecessor, lucky Larry Olsen? Some town in New Jersey. Patterson, perhaps, like the poet Williams. With the time or at least the presence of mind for jotting verses on his prescription pad. Or contemplating a new four-iron. Or buying a Buick. Or meeting his wife for dinner—London broil. Whatever he was doing, he was living like an American.

chapter six

Dear Katest of All Kates,

This military post is sharp, brown, noisy. What bursts of blue exhaust we belch! Commands are shouted, feet march, gears are ground. It's real, it's dependable, it's safe—so long as I don't forget the passwords. They change every day and one is expected to keep au courant, at risk of being shot by Korean sentries who prowl these premises like shabby robots. It's quite a challenge to head for the three-holer at night and hear that nerve-jangling cry: "Haw! Hoo gose deh?" That first 'Haw" gets me every time. Even when I have the password it is driven from my memory like a fish startled by a stone. The words for each day—there are two—are in no way related to each other. Yesterday's were Oak and Splash (Sprash). For the life of me—literally—I can't seem to remember more than one at a time, and it's generally yesterday's. In my frustration several times I have shouted out an epithet that really is the purpose of my outing: "Shit!" How much easier for me if that were the password. At least I haven't heard of anybody getting shot. In all likelihood—I'm counting on it— the poor Korean guards are equally intimidated by the rifles they waggle under my nose while I'm saying things like "Butterfly!" "Tower!" "Chesterfield!" "Eisenhower!" "Please don't shoot!"

I miss you unbearably. Please don't fade.

chapter seven

He watched the seasons change, each one bringing its discomforts, its slender filament of joy, the latter remembered from some distant place. Is the snow heavy on the leaning pine? It is like Maine: stark, haughty, idolized Maine. Are the hills burning with pink jindala? Well, the lilac flounces near the corner of the house, then spends its life out in scent and dies in ecstasy in the backyard. Are the cuckoo blowing oboe-low, the heron stepping *en pointe* in the paddies? He would give his life for a cardinal, an undisciplined bluejay, the iridescent breast of a mourning dove, the shy orioles spinning like moonlets in the tops of the elms.

It was more than homesickness, it was fear mixed with bigotry. Deep down in him there was a cheapness to life here and he knew that it was the distance made it so. Everything that wasn't his made it cheap: their food, their clothing, their houses, this land where no plant of his own could grow for more than a season—the roots would die of estrangement. His bigotry extended beyond the yellow skin, the black hair, the almond eyes, the Oriental chants full of tremolo and crying. Cuckoo and jindala he did not know either, so they must be hated too. As for the small fleeting traces of joy, better to dwell on the miseries—they were real, hard.

One of these appeared in the small fading mirror that was nailed to the tent post. He turned to study it. This was more than unfortunate, this was pure deprivation. There was a constriction about the nostrils as if held closed against some evil smell. The eyes were heavily lidded, opaque, revealing only enough of their color to avoid a blind stumble. The lips were rolled in and compressed between the teeth, as though to brace the mouth against some liquefying influence. There was an overall sense of disgust about the features. He had an impulse to make a sign and hang it beneath the mirror: AVERSION. He wondered if it was too soon in the day to take a drink. He wondered how long before it would never be too soon.

He turned from the mirror to Kate, sweet Kate.

Dearest Thing I Have,

I read your last to me at least twenty times. I hope you believe me that memories and dreams of your kiss and your touch make me a winner out of all this game. I say "game" because you ask about my superior officers. Well, they aren't superior, they are a gang of psychopaths, scum of the earth who seem to take special pains to reduce everybody to dirt beneath their boots. You ask if it is clean and sanitary. Last night I dreamed that I heard the sound of a toilet flushing, and that was the most glorious sound I've ever heard—at least in a dream.

And yet . . . in spite of all that . . . I think that I am beginning to lose something here: my tourism. There is a safety and a marvelous isolation in being a tourist, a gatherer of impressions, probing the port of call with varying degrees of insouciance. A tourist is like the happy dead: he cannot be touched or drawn in. He sees but is blind, is deaf but he hears—unless, by the bite of a cobra, the crash of an airplane, he is transformed into the substance of the country he visits. Armies are traveling beasts who drop off bits of themselves like waste into alien ground. In my case, however, it is more subtle, more insidious. I feel my nationalism falling away. Korea threatens to drag me into its misery and its mystery. And I am a little frightened.

Tonight, for instance, I heard the most familiar melody—it was taps, but this time it seemed so slow, so measured, so infinitely sad in its connection to battles won and lost, womanless days and nights for all the men who have heard it, that it had become the strangest and most awe-inspiring music in the world. Hearing it here makes it wonderful and terrible. Wonderful because, as I say, it is something that I know—or thought that I have known. Terrible because it has so much to do with human suffering. For the first time I heard it as a lament, a farewell—but a farewell to whom? Perhaps to myself. And here is another letter for you, Kate, that won't be sent because it won't be written.

chapter eight

She was the tallest woman he had seen in Korea. She was led in by the hand like an offering. Or like a kind of royalty. Dressed in billowy white pantaloons beneath a long high-waisted skirt, rubber turned-up itiwa, sleeveless open vest and a bright scarf pinned around her neck, she would have looked quite normal were it not for a face that was frozen in an expression of permanent terror through the bulging of her eyes. The eyes were so perilous that Sloane was ready to run to her, basin in hand, for a deep breath could easily pop them from their sockets. Her nostrils flared wildly and her mouth, drawn back and fixed in a grin, presented the maximum orifice for intake of air. She nonetheless gasped rapidly and shallowly, like a spent runner fighting to pay the debt of oxygen borrowed from her heart and her brain.

He watched Yoon taking a history from her husband, who stepped forward and unpinned the cloth around her neck. Yoon sucked in his breath as the woman's throat was bared. Filling the space between chin and breastbone, forcing the head back, was an enormous rounded eminence the size of a grapefruit. She resembled a startled blowfish. Sloane rose and approached her.

"How long has she had this?"

"Five years, Sir Doc. Only twenty days now all asudden too big."

"Does she have pain?"

Yoon spoke and the woman answered. Shrilling through that dry doorway was a metallic whine, all of the same single note without inflection or accent, as if such a luxury would tax beyond renewal whatever fragile reeds vibrated in her throat.

"No, Sir Doc, no pain. Only cannot breathe. No can swarrow. No can rie down rest, only stand up, sit down."

"Where do they live?"

"He shay walk twenty miles, two days to see ouisa. Sir Doc, he shay prease can fix him wife? Pretty soon die."

Sloane led her to a chair and began to outline the tumor with his fingertips. He tapped the surface hopefully, waiting for the returning vibratory wave that would indicate fluid. Fluid could be withdrawn through a needle to diminish the size of the mass and make surgery feasible. There was no fluid. Sloane had never seen such a goiter. Even in a hospital this would be dangerous, but there was no place to take her, no place to send her. What if there was bleeding from high and behind it, where he could not see to control it? No blood transfusion. No oxygen. What if she could not tolerate the local anesthetic? He had no means to put her to sleep. It would have to be novocaine with the patient wide awake. She would be awake all right.

By the time Sloane had finished his surgical residency his thirst for pathology had been slaked. It was normalcy he craved, normalcy with its clean lines and rounded glistening eminences, the unclouded lens, the white whipslide of a tendon, the airy comb of the lung, elastic, continually refreshed. Still, it was in the ricochet from disease that he was sometimes able, privileged, to see the sad beauty of man, tangentially, on the rebound. To see this sufferer recovered—of course that would please him. But that was far away. "He shay prease can fix him wife?" Well, no, probably not. He

30

could *do his best*, but he knew that even here that was no consolation, not for him, nor would it ever be. From the first time he heard it there was something too easy, too slick even about that oft-repeated phrase, "Well, I did the best I could for her." He always expected, perhaps even hoped for someone to say, "Why wasn't your best better?" and he had promised never to say it. No, there was no way out except to send the woman home and let her die there—or on the way. "Pretty soon die." Her husband had the right diagnosis. And, perhaps, the only way of phrasing it. To say this is your last illness, these are your final days needed the honey of compassion properly expressed through subtlety, nuance. To break the news gently would be harder than to save her.

In the end he simply dared himself to do it.

"Tell her I'll take it out. Tomorrow morning."

The woman, unable to bow, pressed her palms together in gratitude, her expression unchanged. Her husband retreated to the door and out the dispensary to wait in the dusty road.

Sloane did not sleep well. Whether dreaming or awake, he was cramming for the surgery of the thyroid gland, fixing in his mind the exact location of the superior and inferior thyroid arteries, the middle thyroid vein, the recurrent laryngeal nerve. Toward morning he could see a torn artery and he heard the loud and unreachable swishing of blood spurting from it. He saw himself pressing on the tumor to stop the bleeding and suffocating the patient in the attempt. At 7:30 she was lying beneath him on the table, bare to the waist, grinning at the ceiling. A rolled blanket had been thrust transversely beneath her upper back so that her head fell back and rested on the table and the neck presented the tumor to best advantage. For twenty minutes he scrubbed her neck, chest, and chin with warm soapy water while the instruments were soaked in alcohol and laid out. The mass pulsated slightly with her heart-beat, a time bomb awaiting detonation. Alcohol was rubbed into her skin, drapes were laid about the neck, a towel was dropped loosely over her face.

"Jang. Tell her she's going to feel a needle."

The tripartite conversation began. He had become so used to speaking through an intermediary that often he was surprised at a direct and immediate answer to something he said around the base.

"Now another. It's burning now but pretty soon it'll be numb."

God help me to get it out.

"Tell her she can breathe just fine. If she needs more air, she has to raise her left hand off the table and I'll pick up the towel. Does she understand? Sure of that? Here we go. Knife."

From earlobe to earlobe, yes, all the room you can get.

"Clamps. Come on, get in here, get in here. Lightly, lightly, don't press—doesn't take much."

These boys don't know *anything*. I've trusted them too much. How scared they are and I'm scolding. We're all scared. She least of all.

He dissected the skin and overlying tissues off the surface of the tumor upward and down as far as he could. Out of the corner of his eye he saw the left hand stir and falter into the air, just an inch, then, gathering courage, it dropped back.

"Novocaine. Better in a minute. Tell her. Okay, retractors. Hold them like this. No no no goddamn it like *this*."

Ignorant bloody goddamn ignorant *gooks*.

The last thin layer of covering was stripped from the tumor and it bulged nakedly, throbbing, tense with blood. It was purple, crisscrossed with interlacing veins and arteries. With his index finger be began to break up the filmy adhesions between its surface and the adjacent structures. With infinite care he swept his finger to and fro, each time a bit farther. Instantly the wound filled with blood, obscuring the operative field.

"Watch out. Clamp. Clamp. Wipe. Okay, I've got it. Suture."

He controlled the torn vessel with pressure from his finger. Now, still holding it, he passed a stitch into the mass beneath his finger, then again. When he removed his finger the lake of blood reappeared. He tied the first knot, threw down the second and third, wiped the blood away.

"That's got it. Good. Now—let's go."

That first drenching had lowered him into the battle and calmed him. He might be able to do it again if he had to. Now the entire front of the tumor was cleared and he worked around to the sides, peeling away strands of muscle, clamping, ligating, dividing vessels.

"Novocaine."

Giving the anesthetic was an interlude in which he relaxed from the implacable advance of the operation. It carried no danger. He was certain that she enjoyed the respite as much as he.

One by one he located and surrounded the great vessels of the thyroid, passing silk threads beneath them, tying his heart down with each knot. Both superior vessels, then the inferior two. Now it's done. So you really *are* a surgeon, Sloane. Now—start peeling out.

"Watch for the parathyroids. Mustn't take it all. Leave a bit. Boy, look at that trachea." The cartilage rings and the windpipe were compressed, eroded. "No wonder she couldn't breathe. Here we go. One more snip. One. More. *Snip*. It's *out*."

The slippery purple ball lay in his hands. He cradled it for a moment like the heart of a saint, then he set it in a basin.

"Let's wash this out and get out of this neck. Saline, sutures. Dressing—heavy compression but not too tight or she'll choke. All done, mama-san. Good good brave girl."

He squeezed her hand.

A week later, when she left with a bandage in the middle of her throat and her scarf in her hand, she had shrunken somehow, fallen back into the commonplace, but Sloane remembered her as she had been, an empress, tall and stiff and tortured, grinning as she was led about.

chapter nine

Kate My Own,

I dreamt that I was in an empty room. Through a closed door I could hear bursts of applause. Hundreds of people were clapping their hands. It would stop, then start again, as though punctuating a speech that I could not hear. Again and again it rattled forth, rising from separable sounds to a great roar, a blending of mass approbation. I wondered if the applause were for me. I felt self-consciously certain that it was. Had I done something heroic? Would I soon then be summoned to make a triumphant appearance before a cheering multitude? In the next moment I saw that the crowd was applauding for the promise of my punishment. The more horribly it was portrayed, the louder the cheering. Soon the door would be thrust open and I would be dragged to a stage where my torture would be carried out. The mob would applaud for each new bedevilment of my flesh. There was a hand at the door, pushing. I crouched at the far corner of the room, tense, palpitating. And woke up.

Sloane tore up the sheet of stationery and started on another.

My Loved Thing,

There's really nothing to worry about. It is you who has to be careful never to have spaghetti and meatballs again. When I get out of here we've got to be the same people we were when I left. So, no more Italian restaurants for you! As for me, you have kept me toasted when it's cold, damp, and wet, and you have kept me alive when it seems like nothing around me is. But life here in Korea is not horrible. The worst one can say is that it's a little insane, but that's the army for you. At least I am still not minus any buttons. But here is an example of how the army operates: On Sunday mornings we all go to church. Well, My Mouse, "church" is what they call it. This is a large Quonset hut topped by a large wooden cross. Against this, some bored general once saw fit to lay a great stone chimney. Not meant for heat at all, it added an absurd note of elegance to the structure. But then rains came and they came seriously, as they always do, and the chimney washed away downhill. Then, when the bulldozer was clearing the chimney rocks, it ran over and crushed a small dog. So much for Uncle Sam and architectural ornament.

Last Sunday the sermon was all about the Assyrians and divinely inspired generals. Our general sat wholly uninspired in the front row flanked by the automatons officially called aides. The general kept clearing his throat self-righteously, something I wouldn't have thought possible until I heard him doing it. You'll have to take my word for that. The fact that I'm thinking about you all the time—even in church—you'll have to take my word for that too.

Most Sundays the last four rows are filled with Koreans, some of whom walk many miles to come to the service having set out in the dark before dawn. They recognize the hymns by their melodies and after the first few bars they sing along in Korean. If I say that it sounds cacophonic you will think that it sounds like shit but it is worse than that. At least there is only one Sunday in the week, a fact of life that the U.S. Army hasn't been able to mess around with—yet.

Another fact of life is that I'm going to dream of you again tonight.

On his cot in the moments before sleep Sloane was thinking about Columbus, how he kept two journals when he sailed the *Santa Maria*: one for the crew, one for the truth.

chapter ten

Sloane was lancing an abscess when it happened. He saw his hand, holding the scalpel, trembling. At first finely, but it grew into a coarser motion, a shaking no longer even and regular but occasionally flying into a widely swinging jerk. He backed off from the bristling red mound in the middle of the man's back.

"Shut that door! It's colder than hell in here."

"It *is* shut, Sir Doc."

His patient, who was naked to the waist, wasn't shivering.

Take care, Sloane. You're tired. This is just an abscess. Simple, no danger. Calm down.

He tried taking deep breaths, pushing them slowly out, but even his breath quivered, moving in and out in short staccato bursts.

He advanced again upon the abscess. Once more his right hand disobeyed, discharging its movement senselessly, almost epileptiform. He grasped it with his other hand, pressing firmly, and pushed the quivering blade to the apex of the mound. At the last moment it veered crazily off center and stabbed a good half-inch to the side of the lesion. A stripe of useless red appeared where it had struck.

This is more than tired.

What's the matter with me?

He felt heat searing his face and the collar of his shirt was uncomfortably damp. Again he steeled the muscles of his arms and aimed the vibrating blade toward the patient. Never this kind of fear before. He felt threatened. With his whole strength and control he moved ahead with no idea where the capricious knife would choose to land. Then a third hand, brown, cool, hard, swam into his field of vision and closed upon his. Relaxing into passivity, he gave up to this new force and let it take control. The scalpel drove straight to the mark, stabbed, then cut. A line of blood, then a velvety wave of greenish-white pus erupted from the wound in a small geyser. Its pressure spent, it settled down into a steady stream across the man's back. He looked up at Jang and murmured tremulously.

"P—pack it with g—gauze when it stops."

He stood there helplessly as Jang pried his rigid fingers from the knife handle.

"Sir Doc sick. Shaky. Too hot sick. Feber. Too bad sick. No can do sick call."

Sloane did indeed feel himself growing sick, as though Jang's words had freed his illness to manifest itself or had at least brought it to the surface of awareness. Jang's face was a mask of anxiety and gloom.

"We go bed now, Sir Doc."

He put his arm around Sloane, tucking his hand under the armpit and lifting.

"Ah tsk tsk tsk. Sir Doc number ten sick."

Jang helped him to a cot in the dispensary and began removing his clothes. Sloane's entire body shook violently, the metal cot rattling on the floor like a snare drum. Weakness, profound, deep as a well, flooded him and he gave up all hope of self-control. Tears came to his eyes. He tried to talk but his lips seemed to have liquefied and any attempt to speak caused them to flow into the most exaggerated shapes.

"Hoo boy tempature one hundred five," said Yoon reverently. "Too much sick. Maraddia. Give Toeshan chloroquine, rno'skoshi. Rub alcohol all over body. Pretty soon good okay number one."

Sloane heard them discussing his illness and the treatment. Through the weakness and nausea he knew they were right. Malaria. Number ten sick. He lapsed into delirium, giving in to the chill, feeling his flesh flinging itself helter-skelter on the cot. At one point Yoon and Jang, moving on either side, placed their arms across his body to keep him from flopping onto the floor. His voice raged, hoarse, desperate.

"Stop! You're killing me! You fucking gooks! I *hate* you and your fucking no-good fucking country! *Stop* it!"

It was black and he was lying in the shallows. Cold green waves rocked him back and forth, slapping his flesh into frozen weeds. Along came rats on the land and fish in the sea. Between the two they tore him leaf and stem to insignificant vegetation. Sloane thought of an old blues number he had heard on a Victrola at Fort Sam Houston, "Yellow Snake Moan." He was the yellow. He was the snake. He was the moan. Or was it "Black Snake Moan"? He would soon be the black. Bye-bye, boys. Bye-bye, Quonsets. Papa loves mambo, so keep dancing, Kate. Be glad you never saw the kids here, shivering orphans, begging to walk beneath your trenchcoat.

For hours, Yoon and Jang rubbed his sizzling skin with alcohol, fanning the air to hasten evaporation and lower the temperature. He was a naked neon corpse, twitching on and off.

"What it shay?"

"Hundred one. More better now. Can sreep."

Sloane heard the round hollow voices from deep within his head and fell asleep. The next day he was weak, but the fever was moderate. The chloroquine would take hold now. The boys were squatting in a corner and when he awoke they looked at him, smiling.

"Sir Doc talk prenty dirty rast night," said Yoon. "Number ten," and the boys both doubled up, laughing hysterically.

In that sudden fiery episode Sloane had yielded his membership in the ranks of the doers and was forced to accept a seat in the audience. Without the security of his health he had felt his manliness recede. In one respect, though, it was a kind of advance, for with this act of resignation came an increased awareness and acceptance of his fellows. Their motives, their discomforts, their downright sufferings became matters of notice in which he started to see small pieces of himself. Not that it made him feel any stronger. He was ill at ease almost all the time now, the fever on a low burner, capable at any moment of flaring and laying him low for days at a time. He was often forced to stagger on his rounds, weighty and limp. Slight anxieties such as arose in cases of moderate complexity were enough to sap his small reserves, leaving him dizzy, his skin thrilling to waves of fever. In moments of real stress—in difficult surgeries or childbirth—his shallow quick breath would come bursting against his clenched teeth and in his chest a fluttering as though a deck of cards were being shuffled beneath his breastbone. He slowly increased the dose of chloroquine but that increased his depression, making it harder to summon the will to get up in the morning and face sick call. He was often unable to eat, his alimentary apparatus lying slumped in lethargy, wholly unwilling to lumber into activity—to moisten, to lubricate, to grind, to mix, to peristalse. "It is too much," he heard it saying and he agreed. Between the malaria and the depression his weight loss left him without an once of reserve.

They were sitting in the dispensary. The patients had left and the boys were washing the instruments. The nightly fever was rising quickly in Sloane's head. It made him restless and bored at the same time and, as usual, too tired to move.

"Jang. Tell me a story."

"Sir Doc?"

"Don't you know any stories?"

"Ah, Sir Doc. Shtory. Laugh shtory?"

"Story—any story about Korea."

There was a brief conference with Yoon, much disagreement, a few false laughing starts, and Jang began.

"One time a too poor old man from my virrage, he shee a too small bird fall down nest. Too bad sick, break reg. He say 'ah-ah' and he pickem up his hand, rike this, takee his house. After a while he takee shtick, make a shprint, hmm? Fixem on birdie reg with shtring. Birdie so happy, get all better, pretty soon fry away, bye-bye. Birdie fry a rong rong time. Faraway prace. Cheju Irand, where King of Birdies stay. He tell King of Birdies man put shprint in his reg, make all better. King shay, 'Number one man. I rikee too much,' and he cry, good happy. Then he shay birdie, 'Go back to nice man garden, put gold in alla gourd on roof.' Birdie do, bye-bye. Man cut open gourds, *all* furra gold. Old man too happy. Now."

Jang waggled a finger sternly.

"Nice man have bad number ten friend rive next house. He too mean man. He shpy, shneaky, find out. Ohhhh. Gold! So. He go his own garden, catchee rittle birdie, break her reg."

Jang snapped the leg.

"Then he take shtick, make a shprint, hmm? Then he takee house. Pretty soon birdie all better, fry away, bye-bye. She fry Cheju Irand, tell King of Birdies man break reg, after put shprint. King shay, 'Number ten. No rike mean man. Go back mean man house. He shee you, he cut open gourds on roof.' So, birdie go back, bye-bye, mean man so too grad. Gold! Gold! Gold! Crimb roof, takee alla gourd down, cut-tem open. Every one furra shit!"

With great effort Sloane struggled to his feet and went to his tent. He could hear the boys laughing long after he laid down.

文

Sloane struggled up on one elbow to guess at the time. He was listening to the metallic buzzing of a fly. It had awakened him from a damp, agitated sleep. The noise would stop now and then and he would feel it scuttling through his hair and behind his hot ears, crawling, itching. Each time he reached up to swat it his head would echo feverishly from the blow but the buzzing and itching would instantly resume. He felt he might go quite violently mad from it. He clenched his fists at his side and lay still, trying another tack: giving in to the torture of the insect. He would let the heat and the itch and the crawl and the buzz roll around his head, drain him to the dregs, then perhaps it would lose its zest for such a flaccid host and wing off to a livelier scene.

It didn't work.

He sat up abruptly, tearing at his hair, rubbing his ears fiercely, clawing at his neck, feeling the pain of his nails and the moisture of the blood they produced. The crawling stopped but the buzz was there, loud, probing his ears, first one, then the other, and suddenly Sloane knew why he couldn't get rid of the fly. Something had happened in his brain and whatever it was had contracted into a green-gold body with busy wings. For a long time it had perched there on the floor of his skull, then it had crawled out his ear and now it swung about his head, fiendish, unswattable—short of lobotomy. He was torn between wanting it to crawl back into his head where at least he wouldn't have to feel it on him, and wanting to thrust his head under water and hold it there until either it stopped or he did.

Sloane watched the skaters flowing across the ice, the list of their knees, the lilt of their shoulders, each with a puff of steamy breath at his lips. Healthy, strong, buoyant, they seemed immortal, like gods at play, and as the fever fed him he saw himself shuffling between these skaters and the bluish-white gaspers of the dispensary, the frailest of his patients desperately in need of what was here in abundance.

How hungry are the heart and the brain when the lungs can find no air for them. Cell after cell swells up and bursts with a kind of silent implosion, until enough are dead so that the rest, pulled into captivity, follow suit with resignation automatically, blackening.

Was there not a bit of breath he could take back with him? Just a droplet of air for each empty lung? Something to whisper into an ear?

Of course he would have to beg for them, these scraps of healing spirit, but he was willing to do that. A master of vertigo—at least of his own—Sloane was able to gauge, from the moment it came upon him, just how far and how fast he'd be able to turn his head from side to side without steepening the falling sensation and inviting the nausea that was so debilitating. He had learned that there was even a way to walk without the nausea claiming him entirely. If only he could stand, make his way across the stern glass of ice without breaking the sack of bones to which he had dwindled. Safer, he thought, to fly to the skaters, avoid the ice entirely. If one can fly in Chagall and other dreams, why not this one, the one called Korea? Then all you would do is drop your hand down to each of them, palm facing upward. "Moment sir—for the love of God—a little breath please?"

After all, the very air that we breathe, the wind itself—isn't that the breath of P'an Ku, the great horned dwarf who, with his mallet and chisel, pounded and chipped the rude masses of matter into the shape of the world before he settled, literally, into his masterpiece so that his voice became thunder, his left eye the sun, his right eye the moon, his veins and muscles the strata of the earth, his flesh the soil, his sweat the rain . . . and the lice upon his body—man? For them to give me a breath is to model themselves after the great Son of Heaven, an act of piety as well as of mercy.

43

But, Sloane wondered, what if he did well with his begging? Shouldn't he have a breath basket? Ask the boys to make him one. They would know how. They would weave it out of the ice and the dust and that other kind of healing that preceded his by a few thousand years.

Sloane wondered whether he had told . . . Kate—had he told *Kate* about the skaters? Of course she would want him to breath-beg for himself, so he couldn't mention *that*. But then, she didn't know he was sick, did she? She didn't know, even, *who* was sick. How could she? She was *on the other side*. If he told her that, she would probably think that he was talking about the other side of the world. No. Geography! Huh. That was trivial now. What he meant was the other side of life.

His eyes turned as each one smiled by. It was beautifully dizzying. But they were too polite. He could see that they wanted to sweep him up, carry him aloft as they flew, but they would never take the risk of offending him. More than once he closed his eyes for half a minute, hoping that would serve as a signal of his willingness, his longing, but no, they did not understand. And so there he sat, counting the breaths he could take for his patients.

chapter eleven

They were walking home after a round of house calls in the village. Jang and Yoon were ahead of him with the bags. He watched them idly through half-closed lids. They walked side by side. Without warning, one would step aside to get momentum, then crash into the other as if to knock him off the road. Sloane could hear them laughing, spitting, cursing. Children. Babies. Sometimes Sloane talked to them during sick call.

"Jang, these big white birds we see in the rice paddies, the ones with long legs. What do you call them?"

"They call hak, sir."

"Hak?"

They would always giggle when he attempted a word in Korean. Sometimes he did it on purpose to make them silly.

"Hak, sir. He rive rong time. He verrrry old man. More than seventy. Korean people shay hak he mean rong rife. If you catch hak you rive rong rifetime."

One day a little girl carried in a large bouquet of pink jindala. Yoon put it in a water bottle at Sloane's request and stood looking at it dreamily, lifting the petals gently on his fingertips.

"How long does it last?" Sloane asked him.

Yoon shook his head. Sloane was amazed to see tears in his eyes.

"Too very short. Couple days. Everybody shay jindala blood of young young lovers, spattered on mountain. Pretty soon sink in ground, dead."

He thought of these things as he followed them along the road. Suddenly Jang stopped, set down the satchel, grabbed Yoon by the arm, and pointed down the road. In a second they were babbling to each other, smiling, their eyes lit, eager.

"What is it?"

For the first time neither one answered. They seemed wholly absorbed, thrilled out of themselves by what they were watching.

"What's going *on* over there?"

Yoon said, "Rock fight, Sir Doc."

"Rock fight?"

Yoon nodded eagerly.

"Korean peoples do sometime. Is game. Rine up, throw rocks."

"At who?"

"At who wants fight other side."

"At *each other?*"

They laughed, nodding furiously.

"Why?"

Yoon shrugged and covered his mouth.

"That's crazy," Sloane said. "They'll get hurt. You can be blinded, you can be maimed, you can be killed by a rock, even a small one."

More laughter, then a turning away again toward something even stronger than their allegiance to him.

Animals, he thought. A streak of cruelty just barely beneath the skin. These are fine people, Sloane, but just don't *ever* forget who and what you're dealing with.

Shielding his eyes from the sun, he looked down the road. About two hundred yards away a cluster of people had organized into two groups on opposite sides of the road. They were separated by about fifty yards. They were not unlike players waiting their turn. In one group Sloane saw a man whom he had treated at the dispensary some weeks ago for an abscess of the leg. The man had suffered the ministrations with dignity, never expressing by the slightest sign that there was pain. When the draining was done, he had bowed and smiled, backing to the door. Now he stood erect, swaggering, a billow to his pantaloons. In each hand be hefted a large rock. He was smiling and full of pep as he turned to laugh with his friends. Here on his home ground there was none of the deference he had shown in the dispensary, only an easiness like that of the athlete who knows and loves his powers and longs to try them.

Sloane did not see the first throw. Or he might have and thought it was a bird that swooped low across the road. There was no flurry of rocks that followed, only a slow measured pace. Astonished, Sloane found it stimulating to watch the rocks leaping across the road. A movement at his side brought him back to Jang and Yoon loping toward the rock fighters, at the last minute separating each to a different team. From where he crouched behind a cover of trees he could see them lifting rocks, throwing them at each other, and he could see the boys' faces, no longer laughing but wary, hostile, tight-lipped. Enemies. He wondered whether in some secret way they were enemies all the time. Wondered whether it might be said of all friends, all brothers, all men. Wondered whether this was a little war, a way of saying that we don't need artificial borders, international powers, violations of sovereignty, machine-guns, tanks and artillery to fight, we can fight just as well against the men next door, men we ate with this morning. On the other hand it was obvious that they didn't want to kill each other, they wanted to hit each other. And there was no question that they were enjoying themselves.

There was a gracefulness to it.

Such a simple, old act.

It must have been for that, to pick up and throw a rock, that the thumb migrated from the line of the fingers and turned to oppose them. Then man stood up straight in order to throw better than he could on all fours.

Rock throwing. Since leaving his childhood, where the bad boys did it and were scolded about it—"Do you want to knock someone's eye out?"—Sloane had never thought about it. It was fundamental, and seeing it now not for the hunt, not for rage, not for jealousy or justice or even for war but for the elemental enjoyment of it, an act as old as one's species—how is it, he wondered, that we have *stopped* throwing rocks? Why this embarrassment?

Sloane slipped from behind his cover and ran eagerly toward the fight. He joined the group that he had counted as having fewer men and, stooping, picked up a rock. He leaned back on his right leg, his left leg raised straight ahead, and pulling his arm back to the limit he poured all his strength, concentrated, purified, into the rock, which flew without trajectory into the line opposite. The others were throwing faster now, firing one after the other. He could hear the stones thudding into the ground. Now and then a thud would be followed by a wail, "Aie! Aie!" and a cheer from across the road. Again and again his liberated arm threw thunderbolts, the clean sweat pouring down his shoulder blades, the smooth head of the humerus swiveling easily in its socket. The grunt that came from his chest at the moment of discharge was a beautiful sound to him, shockingly strong, healthy, a man-sound and yet animal. He did not see that one of his rocks had struck with telling effect, and where eight had stood now seven remained, plus a muddy heap from which a tongue of blood licked across a discarded Oriental mask. Blinded by the surging of energy within him, he would have thrown forever if Jang had not caught his arm.

"Sir Doc, all done, no more rock fight. Yoon hurt bad."

Sloane stood panting, tousled, legs apart. The rock in his hands fell dully to the ground. As the other wounded were carried off, Jang led him across the road to where Yoon lay on his back.

"Who hit him?" Sloane asked.

"You, Sir Doc. You."

There was no malice in Jang's voice. Why would there be? This is what happens in rock fighting. One side hits the other. A rock doesn't cease to be a rock when its mark is a friend. Was there, he wondered, a trace of congratulation in Jang's voice? In this very old land does a man throw rocks at his father as well, and would he be congratulated for finding him like this?

Both of Yoon's lips had been split in two, the halves of the mouth falling away in a permanent purple grimace. The nose was a torn and twisted mound without visible nostrils. A star-shaped wound with its center just above the middle of the upper lip, radiating outward to the cheeks, oozed blood in a folding, wavy-smooth sheet. It went to join the pile of black clot upon which Yoon's small thin head rested. He looked as though someone had laid a poinsettia on his face.

Sloane took the boy's hand and pressed it to his lips, feeling that clear vision dusting up already. Later he tried to describe it: *clouding up with civilization.* It was awkward but accurate, even if no one else would know what he meant. Not that he would ever speak about it. If this had been madness, then he—or at least a part of him—had encouraged and approved of it, even reveled in it, fevered on it. This other Sloane that slept within him, awakened by a rock— was he his mother's son too, or was he born elsewhere?

At the dispensary he washed and debrided the wounds and sutured them impeccably. It wasn't part of the game. And one doesn't doctor with a rock. Afterward he walked to the outhouse and vomited long and eagerly.

For two weeks following the rock fight Sloane did not dream, or if there were dreams he could not remember them. On Yoon's first day back to work, Yoon gave Sloane an embarrassed smile, a smile as though they had shared something secret, furtive, but pleasurable, like sex. Sloane could see the absence of teeth as a blackness between the crooked lips. That night the dreaming returned.

chapter twelve

After three months he had seen nothing of the war. Now and then on a hillside he would find vestiges of it—a scatter of craters or the carcass of a tank twisted and rusting like a plated dinosaur—and he would wonder at their antiquity, wonder what warriors had left them. Then one morning Sloane awoke to the presence of battle. He knew it from the first tentative sniffing of the air, a mixture of oil, blood, sulphur, and a richer smell like that of flesh liquefying into the ground. Gears were grinding, men shouted, and a wild blare rolled back and forth across the air. Bombs, shells, machine-gun fire, zing and bunk-bunk ratta-tatta—boom! They never saw the enemy. With no corpus against which to marshal one's energy one could listen only and heard too late the sex-less whine of his own missile and suddenly there are flames in the tangled willows. Compared to this, hand-to-hand combat must have been a kind of lovemaking.

When the first three casualties appeared at the dispensary they were like biblical visitors presenting their wounds as though they were jewels, rich bursts of red flesh gingerly held out by their bearers.

Sloane stood amid the stretchers, dazzled at their costliness.

Beneath one blanket a spike of bone pointed through torn muscles. The boy's face was moon-white, his leg flailed helplessly as he was lifted to a cot, and through his open shirtfront the narrow neck was ridged by an Adam's apple bobbing slowly up and down. The second man was holding something on his stomach with both hands as though it were a cat that might leap off. Sloane loosened the bandage and peered between the cupped hands. A floral pattern of intestine wound sinuously between the fingers. From beneath an eyepatch festoons of clotted black blood looped the cheek of the third man.

"Soak it off with peroxide," Sloane ordered, and the loosened patch gave suddenly with a sucking sound. Still stuck to it came the torn and empty globule that was the eye.

爻

Sloane pointed to the boy with the abdominal wound.

"That one first. Send ahead that we *cannot* handle *any* more majors for six hours. It'll take that long for these three. Six hours. *At least.* Tell them to send *everyone* they can on to Ui Jong Bu *if possible*. Otherwise, we'll take them, but *only* the minors. They *must* give us six hours."

The boy with the belly wound was lifted to the high wooden table. Sloane punched open a can of ether and started dripping it into a cone over his face.

"Breathe deeply. Blow it away. Don't fret. You're safe now. I'm not going to let *anything* happen to you. When you wake up you'll be fine, just fine. *Trust that.*"

He dripped the ether until the hands holding the intestines fell softly away to the sides.

"Here, Jang. Drip this. *Slowly.* One drop every three seconds. One drop, three seconds. No more, no less. You get it? *One* drop every *three.*"

Jang nodded eagerly and began to pour the ether. Sloane watched him for a moment.

"Not so fast. Too fast, no good. You be careful or I'll get someone else." As though there *were* someone else.

"Pour that alcohol. Hands and my arms. There—that's enough."

He rubbed his hands together fiercely, cleaning under nails with other nails. He was thinking about the inside of the abdomen and what he would find there when he entered.

"Now more."

He splashed the alcohol over his arms and let it drip off his elbows. "Again. All right, now the instruments."

At each order the men jolted into action. He saw how clumsy they were, naive, driven into automaticity by their awe of that pink and crawling loop of bowel, their own nearness to it. He scrubbed the abdominal wall around the wound with soapy water and outlined a rectangle of skin with towels. Inserting his index finger into the wound alongside the intestine, he drew the scalpel down across the abdomen. A bloody stripe appeared. He stroked again with the blade. The yellow fat lay parted at the base. Again, then again until the stray loop was joined by its fellows. He inserted the retractors.

"Hold these just like this."

Yoon took them.

"Pull harder."

Yoon pulled.

"Now don't move until I tell you. Good. Bring the other light over. *Come on*—bring it *over*."

He was barehanded as usual. Long since, he had run out of rubber gloves. He grasped the bowel and began to withdraw it. He would have to examine every inch of it, making sure there was no perforation. Let there be no leakage of feces, no hole in the gut please. Otherwise he'd have to resect the pieces, stitch the severed ends together. When the pile of intestines outside the body had grown to a large mound hanging from the incision, he could feel his assistants watching him in horror. Slowly he surveyed the surface of the bowel, running it between the thumb and fingers of one hand, turning it to examine the under-surface. No odor of feces, no hole. His hand dipped into the cleft, feeling for any interruption in the smooth contour of the organs. Spleen. Left kidney. Colon. Bladder. Then around to the right kidney, his hand now immersed in the abdomen almost up to the elbow. Liver. Stomach. Now to replace the bowel.

"Lift high and hard. Up to the ceiling."

The bowel began to slip wetly out of sight.

"Look out, he's waking up. Pour, dammit—*faster*."

The muscles of the abdominal wall tightened and the bowel threw itself up and out of the wound. He leaned on it with his hand, trying to hold it in. A large coil escaped between his fingers and fell across the back of his arm.

"Pour. Pour faster. Get him *down*, he's going to *vomit*. Turn his head to the side. Hold it, keep it down. *Don't* let him *choke*. Now pour, *please*, pour goddamnitall. Never mind the mess."

He felt the boy's body loosening again, sliding into unconsciousness, the edges of the wound relaxing.

"Keep going."

With infinite care he replaced loop after loop.

"Lift harder."

It was all in.

"Let's have the sutures."

When it was done he said, "You are good good boys. Number one. Put him to bed. Wash the table. Get the next."

He pointed to the eye wound. The youth's uncovered eye followed his movements, swinging from his hands to his face.

"Peroxide. Pour it slowly on the gauze."

He gently irrigated the eye socket, wiping away clots, picking out loose stringy ends of tissue, bits of vegetation that had been driven in. There was bleeding at the base, too much to let alone. This is going to hurt.

"Hold his arms and his legs. Grab his head, too. Tight. Hold it tighter. *Tighter*. He mustn't move."

He leaned down and breathed into the boy's ear, close enough for his lips to touch.

"Okay now, it's going to hurt. Try to keep still. Really try. I'll be quick."

He prepared the sutures, threading the black thread through the eye of a curved needle, then fitting it into the jaws of the hemostat.

"Now. *All* of you. *Hold* him. Tight. Understand? *No movement*. Tied down tight."

He mopped the bloody pool out, pressing vigorously, no longer tender. The body stiffened, became rigid but did not struggle. When he had the spurter in view he sank the needle into the tissues around it, pulled it through, then sank it again in a figure of eight. The other eye was shut now, turned in upon a screaming brain, shutting out the world, utterly absorbed in the private agony. He tied the first knot. That's got it. Then the second and the third.

"Now pour again."

It was washed clean. There was no fresh bleeding.

"Ointment."

He emptied the tube of aureomycin into the socket, filling it to the brim, packing gauze squares on top of it for pressure.

"Put a bandage over it, round and round the head. Leave his ear *out*. Would *you* like to have an ear *squashed* like that? Put him to bed. Clean up, get the next one ready."

He stepped out of the Quonset hut and headed for the outhouse, the demands of foreign amoebae tunneling into his bowel. The night was full of bellowing and bumping. Strange that he had heard nothing inside. He had a period of weakness as the diarrhea took him. The cramps, the odor, the sweating all over, the bruised and burning hemorrhoids, the sight and the thought of where he was. Living or dying or even fighting in a place is not the same as being sick there. Dysentery and malaria had combined to establish a kinship of disease between the Koreans and himself. It drove them together. Perhaps therein lay the solution to the struggle of ideologies, he thought. Give both sides amoebiasis, give them malaria, give them a common ground of suffering with neither the time nor the energy for war.

He bent forward and put his head between his knees until it passed. At least it waited until now. At least no one else came to join him. Often he had to suffer with a man on each side of him. When all three were sick, the place was unbreathable. With his eyes closed he started to dream a little but then he roused himself to finish. How he would have loved to drop down deeper. "Surgeons are not for sleeping," he was told during his residency. There's a boy out there who is waiting for his leg. In a much better world they would both dream deeply without this duet. As he walked down the hill he had to stop and ask whether that was an aftercramp or whether he needed the three-holer again. The answer turned him around and back up the hill. "It just doesn't end, does it?" he said aloud. Such merciless rejection when the body doesn't want something in it. Not most of it out—*all of it*. It was something he couldn't bluff, something he couldn't argue with, not even if Eisenhower were down there wounded and waiting.

For two hours he cleansed and washed the wound of the third patient, cutting away all the devitalized and contused tissue, chipping at the blackened spicules of bone for a semblance of cleanliness.

"Hold him under the arms and pull. Yoon. Take the foot and pull as hard as you can. We must try to straighten it out. Harder. Now *keep* it that way. Plaster rolls. Bucket of water."

He dipped the rolls one by one and wrapped them snugly about the leg from toes to groin while the Koreans, standing opposite each other, pulled as hard as they could. Over the wound he left a window in the cast to change the dressing.

"A few minutes more till it hardens, then to bed."

There was a new arrival, a young man lying on a stretcher. He had raised himself up on his elbows and was staring down at his crotch with silent fascination. A dark stain covered the entire front of his pants, expanding down the legs. It spread slowly even as he watched. Later Sloane would have to tell him he had lost his testicles.

chapter thirteen

The war withdrew but everyone knew it would come again. Meanwhile, the base settled into middle-class orderliness. Once, when he tried to tell Kate about his fellow officers, he realized how entirely separate he was simply by the nature of his profession. Even in the army, even in a war, even in battle a physician's role is not that of a soldier. Really he was no more a soldier than Kate was a surgeon. *Soldier* and *physician* are antonyms. No, he was not one of them, and sometimes it even felt as if they were his enemy, especially when they disrupted his work for a mindless inspection or a battle alert—known, inexplicably, as a George. Nevertheless, Sloane dined with the officers and, like them, he drank from three to six shots of bourbon between five o'clock and midnight.

Even this depressed recreation was not without its perils and penances. One Saturday night he pulled a chair up to an upright piano that was rotting in a corner of the hut where they gathered. It was nameless, benchless, its keys had no cover, it was missing its high A-flat and it was so out of tune that he spent most of his time trying to find a melody to play without wincing. That was "Swanee." How I love ya how I love ya. The Sloane version was a lot slower than Jolson's. The folks up north will see me no more—that was something a soldier could relate to here. Two officers came and sang it with him. They looked like father and son. They sang it loud, they sang it soft, and for one verse the older man closed his eyes and, drumming the air with a swagger stick, bump-pa-bumped the bass part. A scatter of voices joined in from behind them. Somehow Gershwin's Yiddish vernacular, written atop a Manhattan bus and turned into a hit by a black-face minstrel named Yoleson, was energizing a hut full of warriors on a Korean hillside. Sloane was impressed at how well the song was doing its job. When it was over the piano was out of music.

This entire interlude, which, in retrospect, Sloane placed between his fifth and his last shot of bourbon, could not have lasted more than twenty minutes. But Sloane was observed, note was taken, and next morning an order was sent down that he would play the organ in church on Sunday. Every Sunday. Effective the following week. Sloane was reminded of a Korean proverb that even a fish wouldn't get into trouble if it kept its mouth shut, and now he understood that it even applied to "Swanee" and a broken keyboard. As for Sloane's protestations—that he had never taken a lesson on the keyboard; that he had never touched an organ; that his facility on the piano was restricted to "Swanee," "Red River Valley," and a few of the art songs that his mother had sung in bars; that he did not know one hymn—all of that was considered immaterial. When he told the martinet who delivered the general's orders, "I'm *the furthest thing* from a Sunday organist," the answer came back that on the base he was the closest thing to it, discussion closed.

Another result of that fatal tinkering (why hadn't he gone to bed?) was that he was ordered to "consult" with the chaplain, a grimy little drunk whom Sloane was treating for palpitations, for chronic high blood pressure and, after hours, for venereal disease. Odd, Sloane thought, that he could look at a mangled bloody torso easier than he could look at this pathetic stand-in for the Lord. After struggling through "Abide with Me" and "Blessed Be the Ties that Bind,"

Sloane discovered that "Fairest Lord Jesus" was the easiest for him. Then the chaplain explained that there were cues to be learned and tempos must be kept because the congregation was going to sing along. Sloane's agitation at this prompted the chaplain to say, "Well, you certainly haven't got much patience."

"I have a dispensary that is fucking *full* of patients," Sloane croaked in a low tone. "From which I have been dragged away in order to practice hymns. On the organ. Which I do not play. As a tribute to a Supreme Being in whom I do not believe. In front of a congregation I am going to treat for the clap Monday morning."

Sloane did not include but insinuated the chaplain by pausing long enough for the thought to register.

"So," he continued. "Whoever wants to sing will have to follow *me*. *Or* not. I cannot *possibly* play this *thing* and yet think about *any*body or *any*thing else in the world, least of all the tempo at which we are all praising the Lord for watching over the war, over the wounds in my dispensary, over the bodies blown to smithereens by missiles and land mines, and over the microbes reducing me to a hundred and nine pounds and testing my ability, day in, day out, to make it up the hill to the three-holer *in time*. Which is where I am headed now."

Neither this nor any of Sloane's outbursts appeared to have much effect on the chaplain. During the three sessions in which he was ordered to meet with him in preparation for the trial that Sunday, the chaplain was breathing down his neck quite literally, prompting Sloane to wonder whether the chaplain had convinced himself that supervising the organist who played God's music was compensation for not having supervised himself. Sloane said as much, for he learned rather quickly that the chaplain, so odious to him with his tics and his twitches, his sweaty hands, his fetid breath, was imperturbable by anything as slight as an outburst or an insult. Sloane even found some relief in the fact that he could say almost anything to the chaplain without consequence.

"It is for *my* sins that I am doing this," Sloane said toward the end of the second rehearsal when the chaplain's body odor was running too high to bear. "As for *your sins*, it will take more than drooling into my ears. Why don't you go get a bath?"

Ironic, Sloane thought, that in a country in which half the population does not have apocrine glands—glands that emit odorous substances—here I am enchambered with one of the earth's raunchiest Caucasians.

"It's just that it's better played with a C-sharp minor," the chaplain said. "Won't you at least try it?"

"I don't see why *you* can't play it," Sloane said.

"That's impossible. I have to conduct the service."

"There's a long respected tradition of conducting from the organ."

The chaplain shuffled sheet music to show Sloane proof that the C-sharp minor had to be played.

"Do you happen to know who the first chaplain was?" Sloane asked him.

"Do you mean here, before me?"

"No, I mean before all other chaplains."

"Historically? No."

"He was keeper of the cloak of St. Martin. St. Martin was the first known conscientious objector. In this war my objection is less controversial: I object to playing the organ. I would rather fire a gun. I would be better at it. You, as a chaplain, ought to be protecting me."

"But aren't I?" the chaplain asked. "Aren't I helping you to sound respectable? Why is a C-sharp minor so hard for you to bear?"

"Well, for *now*, *you* can play it," Sloane said, getting up. "*I'm* off to the can again. That'll be all for today. And may the spirit of St. Martin forgive you."

During the pain of the three-holer he tried to blame the chaplain for his dysentery, the war—all the misery of his life in Korea—but he was too weak to work it out properly. He tried to think why he would know the life of St. Martin but the answer was that he wouldn't, so he wondered whether he was making it up.

文

On that first wretched Sunday the voices and the organ were so far apart that they might have been different churches. The chaplain was rancorous with sweat and Sloane was dearly hoping for the relief of an air attack. Monday morning there was a new order: he should attend further rehearsals "to present a more professional appearance in front of the population," and that meant working more closely with the chaplain. He was also directed to "learn and perfect a variety of hymns in order to stimulate a wider range of religious emotion." To this Sloane intended to say yes sir but he heard himself saying something else entirely. The robot messenger reminded him that he was under orders.

"I am taking every order but that one," Sloane said.

"Failure to comply could result in discipline."

"What are you going to do?" Sloane said. "Take me out of this dispensary? That will be a holiday. Start now. If you don't, I've been meaning to place myself on sick leave. I am *terribly* ill and I have the authority. I'll do that tonight. Jang and Yoon can sew up the next disembowelment. They can try. Unless you have a replacement. "

Nothing more was said about discipline. The music improved when Sloane wanted it to improve. He continued to medicate the chaplain's devotions among the Korean whores on condition that the organ was never to be discussed. Sloane was learning that even in the army there were ways to say no. He saw that God was on his side and was saying no too when a wild storm washed the church down the hillside. The bench in which the chaplain stored his sheet music disappeared. The organ was salvaged, but for a while there was no place to put it. One night, after his last bourbon, Sloane gathered up a few of the men, located the organ under a jeep-green tarp, and with a light rain falling they loudly rehearsed "How Firm the Foundation."

PART II

The Lark's Tongue

chapter fourteen

The ascent from the main gate to the dispensary was gradual enough, but Sloane noticed with what effort the Koreans strove to accomplish it. In a place where ordinary tasks seemed hopelessly difficult, far beyond the stamina of the people, the long line of stragglers inevitably managed the climb, although not with the neat click and crunch of the West. Tilting, swaying, sagging, they faltered, even fell, but they always moved on, pushed by the threat of the numbers behind. Once word of Sloane's facility had informed the countryside, the division of the day between Korean and G.I. sick calls had broken down completely. The line was all day every day. Larry Olsen, his predecessor, had been either too inept or too smart to have established a reputation. According to Sloane's superiors—the swaggerers, he called them—making house calls would lower him severely in the eyes of the population. "Let them come to you," was the mantra. "Make it too easy, they won't appreciate it. You're not a servant, you're a gift." But Sloane's house calls only added to the mystique that here was a man, a G.I., you could trust with your wife, your mother, your child.

This morning there was a great weight of silence over the valley. Sloane leaned against the door of the dispensary, watching two soldiers at the gate brusquely pushing away the next in line, holding them back while the gate was being closed. They would always stand there silently a while, watching the fortunate ones who moved on up the road in his direction. In the village they would hold themselves fragile and wilting through another day and night. They would come again the next day, unless that night a tiny weight dropped upon the scale and sank the balance. Such deaths occurred nightly in the village and they were due to the fact that he was only one man, a fact for which he held himself responsible.

The first patients had arrived and were squatting on the ground in clusters. A farmer had already entered with an open wound of the arm from which he brushed flies with a small fan. Over the bowing head Sloane saw a girl of perhaps twenty, her white skirt clean and stiff, the jacket trimmed with a thin strip of brown and gold brocade. She stood three-quarters turned away, gazing back above the crowd to the high distance beyond. There was something about the slender pillar of her neck.

He bent over the man's arm. Deliberately he probed the wound, exploring its recesses. Then he cut away the necrotic infected tissue and applied antibiotic ointment and dressing.

"Come again in three days."

"*Kommapsumnidda.*" Thank you.

The girl entered. She was pale and detached, avoiding his gaze.

"*Ode appumnikka?*" Where does it hurt?

Speaking only a little Korean and slightly better Japanese, his examinations were often like shaking a box to guess what lay inside.

The girl's wrist folded toward her chest. His days were so devoid of beauty that he had all but forgotten it; forgotten, too, that there is a stirring in the body that is not painful. Her movement was wholly dignified. She seemed a lamp of milk glass that shed no rays but kept its cold small paleness within, dolorous and aloof.

"What is your name?"

"Shin Young Hae."

The syllables were breathed out and half drawn back within her.

"*Nanungouisa.* I am the doctor. I must examine your chest."

She loosened her skirt tie and sash and removed the small white jacket. Sloane stood behind the childish shoulders and placed the stethoscope on her back.

It seemed a violation.

For the first time in months he felt something different from the pity that came to him so many times a day. He wanted not to hear, not to know, to keep her outside the pale of disease.

Keep her for himself.

He listened and could hear the blood beating in his ears.

The sudden ferocity of his desire frightened him.

He withdrew his trembling hands, fearful that they might betray him. How preposterous, he thought, that it might be desire. It could only be the fever again.

"Dress."

The order was brusque, so much so that he wondered whether perhaps he was talking to himself.

"You must come again tomorrow. Afternoon. Must come."

The girl stood up and bowed. At the nadir of the bow there was a turn of the head and he felt her eyes upon him for an instant, then the cool opalescence floated from the room.

For Sloane, the laying-on of hands worked both ways in a dynamic equilibrium. He needed to touch his patients as they needed to be touched. Contrary to what Olsen had said to him, and despite what he himself had felt on his arrival, it comforted Sloane to feel the bodies of his patients, the heat in them, the whole gorgeous architecture of them. It was as though the body he was feeling passed into his fingers the strength and courage he needed to make it well. Nor was he stingy with his handling. It was sometimes the only thing he could do. It was the same thing here, with this girl—yes, he could say it honestly if he needed to say it. But he was struck by the fact that he didn't seem to care, didn't need that excuse. For the rest of the day Sloane lanced and drained, listened and percussed, cleaned and dressed. He finished and stood alone in the dispensary in the space where she had stood, where she had leaned, trying to feel her coolness in his hands.

chapter fifteen

She was waiting for him near the gate. Her pale lamp was lit beneath a small tree about one hundred yards from the sentry post. She wore the same air of melancholy detachment he had noted in their previous encounters. His pulse beat tumultuously. The knowledge of her illness lent urgency to his need. That afternoon in the dispensary he had confirmed his suspicions. With a mounting sense of horror he had heard the telltale rales on both sides of her chest. His fingers had tapped out the borders of dullness in the lung tissue not expanded with air. Through the microscope he had seen the tiny flecks of red that were the bacteria of tuberculosis. He sensed that the disease was well along and in a state of rapid advancement. He had touched her then in a different way, curiously at first, then with obvious hunger. Startled, she had arched and bent away like a small wild beast. Then she had seen his quivering mouth and the pain in his face and had held out her hand. Sick and exhausted, they clung together for a moment.

He followed her now along the road, watching the small clouds of dust that rose around her feet as she stepped. In the sunset her silver hairpin glowed like molten metal. The meager traffic on the road was a treadmill turned to a different speed. Here and there a farmer bending beneath an A-frame piled with twigs and branches gathered from the hills for a meal. A red ox led by a rope through its nose ring, scudding at the road with frantic little bursts of sidesteps as it strove to keep up with the loping boy. A cart drawn by a bicycle was stacked with bottles of white rice wine. Shin did not turn to see if he followed. He was ablaze with fever.

Shin turned off the road into a path between water-filled rice paddies. A length of elevated footpaths separated the pools and wound toward the smoky village below. He could see the red sky reflected in the water, dotted by the sprouts of rice. Frogs were beginning their evening cacophony, belching richly in the paddies. The rotten overripe smells of kimchi and night soil were strangely stimulating. The path coiled and uncoiled before them, turning capriciously this way, taking an agonizing backtrack, then plunging forward only to swing tauntingly in a new direction. He felt that he could not bear it, that tantalizing path, that solemn promenade; that he must run, take her hand, lead her into the darkening fields before his strength left him and he was too weak to continue.

They came to the thatched village, a cluster of mushrooms in the deepening gloom with shadowy figures squatting along the path, demons from dreams that were only partially, fleetingly his. Heaps of small red peppers laid out to dry in the sun presented the last dim color. A harmonica wept softly in Korean. She stopped before one of the dark mushrooms and waited for him to draw up to her, then turned into a little U-shaped courtyard. They sat on the veranda-like border of the house and removed their shoes. She waited while he unlaced his heavy boots, then they passed through a sliding paper door and were alone in a darkened room.

In the blackness he could hear her breathing and moved toward the sound. He reached out one hand and missed her. With both of his hands waving and swaying, hoping for contact, he turned stiffly in a half-crouch like an automatic toy and still he could not find her. A hand with no more substance than a moth lit upon his ear, steadying him. The moth slid to his neck, fluttered across his lips, flew away.

She helped him with his clothing, unbuttoning his shirt, loosening his belt.

There was a sudden soft impact on his shoulder as though a cat had leaped upon him.

A yard of hair tumbled across his body.

By now he could see her as a cool luminescence. Coughing slightly, she drew him down upon the mat and laid her head upon his burning skin. At some point the pain might have stopped but the coughing never did.

Next afternoon he had a shaking chill. The abdominal torture returned. As dusk fell he started down the road toward the gate and had an abrupt premonition of his own death, that he would pour out what was left of him in a small Korean hut and he would die there virtually unremembered, invisible. The affair suddenly seemed extraterrestrial, out of humanity. It carried the worst danger of all, the danger of being cut loose. He saw Shin for what she was: a mortally sick peasant girl. He could see her lungs, cavitary, purulent, alive with the microscopic red bacteria. How soon would he be forced to decide that she was too close to death for him to penetrate?

He stood in the road. Someone passed him silently, silent enough to be Death but he knew that it wasn't. Whore, perhaps. Or just some ordinary ghost.

Either he or the world had turned unnaturally cold.

He saw that he must not go. The fact that it was a *must* made him sob with relief.

He turned back toward his tent and he lurched onto the cot, drawing the blankets about his head. He felt a copy of *Stars and Stripes* crackling under his chest but he was too tired to move it. He would go to the village tomorrow night.

For now, for just this one night more, he had to stay alive, and being alive and being a man, being a lover, were incompatible. For now he must sleep.

Sloane sat at his desk in the empty dispensary, exhausted, listening to the noiseless passage of the minutes. Somehow he could sense the deposition of sediment in his arteries, feel them hardening, feel the loss of his memory and the slow clouding of the lenses of his eyes, he could feel the joints of his body growing thick and tight, the fat infiltrating his muscles. He was aware of his own decay. Only a little longer and he would turn to dust. *Before she does,* he thought. *That's how fast it's happening.*

chapter sixteen

Shin waited on the shore of the Han River while he pushed the little high-prowed boat into the water. It scraped harshly on the stones and eased into the comfort of the water. Carrying the wicker basket of food and drink, she stepped over the gunwale and, after setting the basket down in the center, remained standing, holding the rudder lightly in one hand. Sloane gave a vigorous last push and leaped into the boat. With a long pole he pushed them farther out until the current caught them, swinging the prow out and into its path. Shin pushed the rudder experimentally to capture the best direction. They had nothing further to do, only to drift with the current toward the islands at the mouth, then back.

"You are married."

She spoke the words softly. It was not an accusation or an entreaty or a revelation of doubt or an announcement of doom, and it was not quite a question, but she seemed to be easing some response from him. There had been no preparation, no introductory gesture, no clearing of her throat. It was as though the words had lain on the floor of her mouth for weeks, ripening, and at last had slipped between her lips. He knew that their delivery had been costly. He nodded. That was all.

Shin was kneeling by the basket in the whiteness of her dress, the long skirt surmounted by the short open jacket, as devoid of ornament or frill as a nun. He had a fleeting picture of Kate observing her with amused tolerance. Kate was so *uninvolved* in this part of him that she took no interest in it, at least not in his imagination. Except that, warm as broth, she would take the paws of this frightened little beast into her grasp and: "Delicious," she would murmur, noting the closed flat face from which the courage would have long since bolted. *That* would put it all in its proper context for him, reestablish the old order of things, offer a solid footing for his sliding, unstable gait. But here was only Shin, pale as death, saying to him, "You are married."

She opened the basket and poured a cup of t'akju from a stoppered bottle and held it up to him, the other hand resting its fingertips on the forearm. It seemed the most beautiful of gestures, this offering, the one hand giving, the other acting as though to restrain the offer, giving it a delicate dimension that is unknown in the West.

They seldom spoke more than a few words at a time unless they were here on the river. Here she had told him of the village to the north that was home until she was twelve, a village in which she had done one thing as a child: she held a pole to which a string was tied and secured to another pole. Six people worked in a line behind the poles setting six rice shoots simultaneously. Then, at a sign, the poles were advanced a few inches and the next row was set. When she was old enough she took her place in line with the others. She could bend for hours, legs apart, without resting. So could her mother, her grandmother, all the others. And here on the river she had told him about the hum, the strange hum in the distance and the day that it became a roar. Bombs fell and explosions jarred the muddy bottom of the paddy as the planes swept low over the fields. They did not know at first whether to crouch or to fall but stood staring at the planes, the patterns of the bullets, and the flying wreckage of each new explosion.

Twelve of their village lay in the reddening mud.

An uprooted ox lay with its hooves in the air, the tether still held to the nose ring, and from a great hole in its belly intestines were slipping. Already a dog had thrust his muzzle among the coils to lick at them.

In the village four houses were burning fiercely.

People stood in the street, sucking in their breath.

Then they came on foot with guns and bayonets and that night Shin left, alone, crouching her way across the rice field, the flames from burning huts shooting into the black night like volcanoes.

Her parents fled too in a different direction.

It was a long hungry trek to her uncle in Ton Du Chon-ni. When she timidly called his name from the matang, a door slid open and an old man stepped out.

It was a year now since she had come down from the north.

These details did not need to be coaxed out of her, for she was still in awe of them and they were alive in her daily. Sloane was not sure he had needed to hear them. All that she had seen might have made her more mature, but the way that she told it made her even more of a child. In fact there was something about the way she told her story that reminded him of board books with one or two sentences beneath an illustration. He had never met anyone who saw so clearly what she told, or who surrendered so deeply to the hypnotizing power of the past.

He watched her preparing the meal, uncovering brass bowls of cold rice and pickles, unwrapping the long-handled flat spoons. She seemed absorbed in the task, as though she were alone. She was as private as the shadow of the nostrils across her lips, a darkening in the red, subtle, as unduplicable as a signature. At these moments he forgot the illness that had settled there, threatening, encamped like an army. If he had felt that Kate had kept secrets from him, these were secrets that could, at least, be told. If he could know Shin better, it had nothing to do with what she could say about herself. He came to know Shin by moving a little farther inside of her, closing the space between them.

Small waves lapped the boards of the little boat, encouraging its drift. It was an exciting sound, warm and moist like her exhalations.

She told him of her uncle.

A week after her arrival at his house, the old man lay on his mat. He was coughing even then. He was turned to the wall and each time he coughed he would draw up his knees to brace against the pain of the jostle. Sweat covered his face with countless small blisters. Now and then one of them would swell, lean toward its fellows as though making a sudden decision, and coalesce into a larger, heavier bead. This would begin slowly at first, then, gathering speed, roll down his face and into extinction, leaving a shiny wet trail where it had flowed.

"You remember that?" Sloane asked.

"Of course!"

She was almost shocked at the suggestion that she might forget something, even the smallest detail.

"I knew uncle was soon to leave," she said. "Every cough tore flesh from his bones."

She told him of the day she had knelt on the paper floor and wiped his face as she had done many times before. She had dipped a cloth into a small bowl of rice wine and squeezed a few drops into his open flaccid mouth. He did not close his lips and she heard the liquid rattling in his throat. At last she saw his neck rise and fall in the act of swallowing.

On that day Shin covered her mouth and suppressed a quiet cough herself. A little wave of weakness passed through her as she stared at the man on the mat.

She knew she was sick.

During the night her garments were saturated with sweat. She had to rise and change them.

"We were all to die with Korea," she said.

Sloane had learned enough Korean to understand what he heard, but at times he had to wonder whether he heard her correctly.

After a year of nursing her uncle, she finally put down the fan with which she had kept the flies from his face and she went to the house of the chief. The chief sighed, drew his breath in a sharp hiss, and laid his pipe in a long bowl. Then he stood and motioned her to follow. He led the way across the paddies to a hillock on the opposite side of the valley. Looking in all directions and then at the sky and again at the hill, he pointed to a spot halfway up, near a pine tree.

"He will be there. Tonight I shall send my son to stand upon your rooftop and call the Invitation to his Soul, that it may peaceably leave the house. Do not be afraid. Do you have the burial clothes?"

For two weeks, whenever she saw her uncle had fallen into a laborious sleep, she had stealthily taken the hemp material from the shelves and had begun stitching together the burial clothes. At the first sign of his stirring she would fold them and rush to the cupboard. One day as she knelt, stitching the hood, she looked up to find his gaze fixed upon her. Then she noticed a change in him, a slight relaxation of the lines in his face, as though he had solved a mystery. A new and deeper silence came to them. There was nothing left to say, nothing of comfort or complaint nor in fact of this world at all.

The body was wrapped in the burial garments and tied around with seven ropes. Outside on the matang the men were building the coffin of poplar boards. Later they would rub it with beaten hen's egg to give it a lacquer. In an hour the procession was on its way, the coffin pulled on a ritual carriage with a flag bearing her uncle's name. Shin followed with the women whose wailing bounced off the rocky hill and echoed shrilly around her head. The coffin was lowered, foot first, head raised, and settled in that position. She turned away to look across the valley as the earth was tamped down.

From then on, Shin felt her own illness thriving, building freely in her chest, lapping at the soft inner stuff of her. It was as though, having finished with her uncle, it had turned upon her, freely now, unhampered. She did not tell Sloane this, Sloane told himself. She told Sloane how, in the afternoon, she would stand among the gourd vines in the tiny kitchen garden. It was such a small green place where she could see things growing, coloring, where the slow rhythm of Korea ebbed and flowed, this year's growth aging into the soft breastlike earth, to fill it out, thickening its juice for next year's crop. The earth of her garden taught her the wisdom of waiting. At least that was how Sloane understood it. How much of what he understood was his interpretation or his misunderstanding did not much matter. He wanted her all the time and he would have her now in the boat if he could. It was a fact of their life together, perhaps the one that she could most count on, perhaps the only one that was real. And yet she accepted the situation completely—or seemed to. He really didn't know.

She turned to gaze at the mountains high in the distance. The pink mist clung to them like the shimmer over hot embers.

"These are not my mountains," she said. "Now they are."

Sloane finished the t'akju and handed back the cup to her outstretched hand.

"I like it here on the river with you," he said. "But now I need to be with you. I need to be with you."

"Last night," she said, "you were on your back with your arms across your eyes. I was silly. I wanted there to be talking but you were asleep, so I spoke to you in sleeping."

"I didn't hear it. What did you say?"

"I was silly."

"What was it?"

"I said, 'The River Han has ten thousand flashings. Under the dark leaves of the lotus, fish lie breeding. Tomorrow we will carry food there in a wicker box and t'akju for you to drink. I will wind up the silver ribbon of the stream, wind it up in a ball and give it to you. Then, wherever you go, you will see the mist along the cliffs where the white heron nests.'"

Later he asked her to write it down for him, exactly as she told it, and he had it translated. Next time he asked her about it.

"This is a poem that you told me," he said.

"Yes."

"Who wrote this?"

She gestured: he did, she did, they did together.

There was a solemnity about the way she undressed him, loosening his belt, removing his shirt, folding it with infinite care, smoothing it over and over with her hands. At one point she raised the folded khaki shirt to her face and pressed it over her, drawing into herself the smell of it, enjoying his vapor, as though in the absence of his flesh his spirit would do as well. At first he had been impatient to the point of annoyance. These slow rituals made him hard, brutal. When at last she crept to his side his force made her gasp but she made no sound, keeping the envelope of sadness about her. It was this sorrowing kind of lovemaking that now excited him beyond anything he had known.

"Why are you always so sad?"

"Not sad. Not sad. Too happy."

Soon his own lovemaking took on the wisdom and restraint that she seemed to have been born with. Her slim body to him, his ear pressed to her neck, listening to her blood, supporting her upon him, turning her with a delicacy that surprised him, as though they were moving together in a fragile web that any roughness would destroy. Certainly it was not like Kate, all jollity and health . . . Kate, who made love with the clear understanding that she would live forever, that she and Sloane had been gloriously chosen for perfect and endless copulation. On their honeymoon he had thought that she was right but he was not entirely sure he was meant for that eternity. Certainly with Kate he was never one body, and there was never the sense that each ending was the end of everything. Shin seemed always to be using her last breaths. His lengthy kisses all but sucked the heart from her throat. She welcomed the pain and the sweetness that took her, each time, a step closer to her doom.

chapter seventeen

Sloane had left the village rather late. It was dark, moonless. He switched a flashlight on and off to help negotiate a turn and to orient himself in the right direction. It was exhilarating to walk in the dark, unsure of one's footing or one's bearings. It was a groping, aided now and then by an intuitive spark. When he reached the edge of the village and flashed his light along the mound of earth that walled in the rice fields, looking for the path, he was gratified to find it but a few feet away. Climbing the slight embankment, he switched off the light and floated along the path, a disembodied concentrate of blackness, undistinguished from the night. It was absolutely calm. No intrusion of wind, noise, smell. He might have been blind. It was a luxurious perversion of the senses, to listen for the friction of a shoot of rice upon its fellow, to hear the young of the cuckoo flopping in their nest, to become aware of a fog by the air on his face.

He had progressed halfway across the valley, sure now of his direction. The cluster of twinkling lights in the void midway between earth and sky—it was difficult to convince himself that that was his destination. The edges of reality were blurred. Which would endure and which was the dream, the black valley of Korea or the military post in the sky? At a given signal the post could carry him back to Connecticut—

and that gave it its own kind of magic. This other world, the calm Korean night, was not so safe. There was no way back. There was only the groping black present. Perhaps he would lose the flashlight, or the batteries would die. Then the pleasure of blindness—would it be quite so delectable?

The first sound reached his awareness long after he had heard the small thudding noise. It came from somewhere in the rice paddy on his left. A second later he heard the tiny splash of a frog jumping from the water. That was from his right.

He was listening now, awake and quickened.

A low grunting and the slight sizzle of a cigarette arced into the water.

He was walking rapidly with the pulse hammering in his neck. Fear had sprung, a full-grown phantom exactly his size, and had clicked into place in his body. He didn't dare use the flashlight. His nostrils were raised in the air, fighting to control the sound of his breath, breath that was not enough to sustain the heightened heart, the heightened brain. At the sound of the running feet directly ahead of him he was a fainting wild-eyed beast.

He flicked on the flashlight. Five wisp-whiskered faces, their cheekbones and brows heightened by his low-held light, were closed upon him, blocking escape on all sides. They would kill me for my boots alone, he thought. To die here in this mud . . . where the rice would be especially green next year. He wondered whether he had enough time to beg for his life and he wondered whether he had enough breath, enough life left to beg for. Could he save enough air from each gasp for a few words? *What were the words in Korean?* He could see now the glint of metal in the beam of light.

"Nanung ouisa imnidda. I am a doctor, you must not hurt me. My friends in the village will kill you. Tomorrow they will come to see me and they will know."

From somewhere he had drawn the words. He snorted them out hysterically and waited. They, too, had paused and were waiting. He pointed to his boots. He sat down on the ground and took them off. Next he slipped out of his jacket and trousers. He piled the cap and the remainder of his clothing on the ground and waited. They had not moved. Blind and naked, he waited. They waited also. The world was a bomb and it felt as if they were all to be blown up together, tic-tic ten-nine-eight, a few seconds of forever. There was a sudden jolting pain in his temple. He had not seen his assailant raise the rock but he knew at the moment of its contact with his crunching, splitting flesh that they would not kill him. The Koreans did not kill like that. Full of hope, he surrendered to the outpouring of his consciousness and fell from the path into the rancid mud. When he awoke in the dispensary the thought occurred to him that he would need to find another pair of boots *in his size*. Mustn't be too big, mustn't be too small. This necessity would occupy the base for some time. Until then he could not be expected to move an inch. He would rest while the base found him a pair of boots. Hopefully someone had measured his feet.

chapter eighteen

Dearest Only of All,

If my letters are, as you say, too seldom and too short, that is because of the workload here. After a day in the dispensary, a day that is often a night as well, I need all the sleep I can get. You must remember that I am performing surgery under conditions that are far from ideal. Often I am doing the work of half a dozen physicians and with no properly trained help at all.

You see, what is wrong here is that I must be doing something right, for the crowds of patients have come to resemble the Last Judgment. On any given day you cannot see the end of it. G.I. sick call? The longer I make the Koreans wait, the longer I have to remain in the dispensary, and so I have had to grow an extra pair of hands in order to treat the afflicted of two nations simultaneously. So, no room for dozing here. Sleep is essential.

Take tonight, for instance. I told you about the Georges, the oddly named attack alerts. They are exercises—as if we needed them—and they are supposed to be sprung upon us without warning, but tonight I've been told through the grapevine that we'll be having one before dawn, so I've got to get some sleep so I can act like a soldier when the time comes. After which, a full day's work!

Also, many's the time I have started to write to you, or wanted to write to you, when I recall there are foolish reports that must be written. It is, after all, the army don't forget. But don't you know that I am thinking of you constantly? Plus, I wish you could read all the wonderful long letters I am writing, in my head, as I work. Masterpieces of the epistolary art.

You say that even my handwriting is different. I hadn't noticed. I had a little bug a while ago that might have given me a shake, but if so, it was imperceptible to me. My two Korean assistants, Jang and Yoon, have never mentioned it. It is touching to me that you noticed—it brings you so close to me and shows me that you still understand me perfectly. You must know then, too, that I am counting the days until we see each other again. I never want to be away from you for this long again—ever. You hear?

That is wonderful news about the antiquing. That old guy who tried to swank you around—he probably sized you up and made you his mark, but little did he know what a bargainer you are! I recall how you handled that snit at the hotel when she added another night to the bill—do you remember? "She's a cool one," I thought with admiration. I will bet that old fart has still not recovered, and wonders how he let go of that vase so cheaply. Your encounter with the two homosexuals is so well rendered that it makes me wonder whether you oughtn't to be a writer. Did they really give you the frames for free? What marvels you will have to show me when I return—but will there be room for all of it? I shall have to have my own practice soon, be very very successful and move us into a mansion at the top of a hill.

With each sentence Sloane fought a wave of nausea. His letters too short! She would never know the cost to him of filling a single sheet. It was a violation of all that he had become to have to create these artificial assemblages, lifeless reconstructions of a Sloane who was lost now forever. He hated that Sloane, for it was a Sloane who had never slept with Shin, a Sloane who would not understand what it meant to be so on fire that he would burn down, easily, everything that stood between him and the soft warm center that was Shin.

Sloane stared into nowhere and waited for the pain to pass through his skull. He could feel it in his teeth. Since the assault, there was never a morning or an afternoon in which he didn't feel it half a dozen times. He could have used the injury to leave this place forever, but that would be to leave Shin forever, and thus the possibility contradicted itself. Ironic, he thought. Now that I can go you couldn't drag me away. Besides, what would become of his patients? To leave now was out of the question.

He folded the letter, placed it in the envelope and licked it closed. After he wrote the return address he looked at both names, that of a man named Sloane and a woman named Sloane. He supposed they would tell him that the woman was his wife. He supposed she would think that he was her husband. He supposed that if he ever returned to the States he would have to behave accordingly. Looking at the envelope, Sloane was looking at a world gone mad.

chapter nineteen

"What time is it?"

The weariness flattened his voice, muffled it so that it was indistinct even to his own ears. When no answer came, he stepped from the door of the dispensary and stared down at the road. He knew she was there waiting for him around the bend, wiping her cheeks now and again with a piece of folded cloth. It was a little worrying gesture, like wringing one's hands or a deep, breath-catching sigh.

For the past two hours, as the line of patients shortened, he had fought against the thought of her. He had gone through the mechanics of sick call, listening to the telling of symptoms, the examinations, the treatments, and all the while the white speck that was Shin was growing larger, taking up more of his consciousness. With the departing bow of the last patient his whole brain would be filled with her, not another bit of room. No one had ever done this to him. It was the start of his life. It was a usurpation, implacable but always perfectly timed, as though she held back her nearness until the patients had all been seen, waiting her turn, knowing that he would come.

"I'm leaving."

"Okay, Sir Doc."

He started down the road but stopped at a burst of loud laughter from the dispensary. In sudden fury he turned to retrace his steps, then he stopped as the men's voices became audible.

"Doc's dippin' his wick tonight."

"No, sir!"

That was Jang.

"Aw cut it out, Jang. You know fuckin well Doc's goin down the village, goin to see his moose. Meets her down the road every night for Christ's sake. Lil piece of it, hmm? *You've* seen her. *I'd* take it too. Shee-*it* that's a sweet babydoll."

"No, Sir!"

Jang's voice was harder now, almost angry.

"Jang—what the hell do *you* care? Even Doc's got to have a little push-push now'n then. And Doc's got the pick a the pack. Good *mornin* lil schoolgirl!"

Sloane could imagine the lewd descriptive gestures. It was a lug named Rogers, a clerk. Aptly named, Sloane thought, for that was all he thought about. As a clerk he was utterly useless. Sloane would find a way of getting even with him—secretly, the bastard.

"What—you don't think he's entitled? *Everyone's* entitled nookie-nookie. Specially a shithole like this one."

"You shut ups!" barked Jang, and Sloane heard the defiant stamp of boots across the floor. Jang was going to fight for him. He had done it before. Right, then—*let* Jang hit the son of a bitch—serves him right. Jang was by far the strongest one in the company. Not the largest or the most muscular but the most to contend with. Slow to anger, and then only on Sloane's account, but with those murderous fists. He had watched Jang settle an account with another Korean soldier. Jang had called to him, a staccato barking sound that the other recognized as a threat or insult, stepping up to accept the challenge. It had been a very workmanlike display of strength and fury. The other man never landed a blow. Sloane had let Jang hit him three times and then yelled from his window. He had felt pleasure in the comfort of Jang's strength and of his friendship. How many people had someone who would die for them?

When the talking stopped abruptly he realized that he had been noticed and a signal had been sent man to man. He stepped inside.

"Rogers."

"Sir?"

"Did you need me for something?"

"No, sir!"

"I'll be with my friends in the village if you need me."

"Yes, sir!"

"In case you think of something you want to say to me."

"Yes, sir!"

"Meanwhile, I should like, just one time, Rogers, to leave this dispensary without having to hear you shoot your dirty brains off."

"Yes, sir! Sorry, sir!"

"If I hear it ever again they might be shot off permanently. I know just the place and I can arrange it."

"Yes, sir!"

This time the *sir* vibrated like a metal rod.

"I left here once. Now I have to leave again. You're the reason why."

"Yes, sir! Sorry, sir!"

"If Jang puts a fist in a face, *I* never saw it, because Jang would never do such a thing, but if he does, that face doesn't work anymore."

"Yes, sir!"

"It disappears under the blows."

"Yes, sir!"

"And it won't be treated in this dispensary."

"Yes, sir!"

Sloane needed to say more, do more, but he stopped himself and turned, hating himself for having spoken at all. In such a situation even a show of strength was a weakness. Halfway down the hill he again heard laughter. Why hadn't he left the matter to Jang? Perhaps now it would happen if he didn't turn around. He continued into the valley to Shin.

文

She was standing beneath an old knobby pine, all of whose branches reached away from the road toward the rice fields beyond, as though entreating the other green things not to abandon it. She stood behind the tree, her back to the road, leaning against it. Sloane spoke softly so as not to startle her. She turned unsmiling, serene. The wheel had turned again and they had come together again. Each time they met it was like that—a stroke of great good luck, a miracle that might not ever happen again. They walked together, sensing each other's relief.

Usually it was after dark when he entered the village, and although everyone knew he was there in the hut, the fact of not having been seen was somehow insulating. This time the sun had not set as they walked silently along, their faces downcast. Out of the corner of his eye, Sloane saw the familiar faces of his patients watching them, some concealing smiles behind their hands, others stony-faced, severe. Sloane knew she was suffering on his account, paying the whole price while he was getting off scot-free. The Koreans hated her because of him and would happily have stoned her were it not for his presence on the hill and their need of him, a need that was absolute. What the whores were doing was not as bad as her offense, which was repugnant to them precisely because she was *not* a whore but one of them, a working peasant, and so all the more a traitor to her people. She bore their scorn in silence, outwardly ignoring the muttered curses, the undisguised contempt. His cheeks burned for her. He wanted to put his arm around her waist and lead her along but he did not have the courage.

There was a commotion in the matang of one of the huts, a three-sided one with stone walls, the home of a wealthy farmer. A small group of people were huddled around a construction of some kind. Two of them were beating it with heavy sticks. He stopped directly in front of the matang. With mounting horror he saw that two poles had been sunk into the ground about three feet apart. Between these two poles there had been strung a dog, its tail and hind legs tied to one, its head and forepaws to the other. It was alive, its mouth hanging weakly open, drops of saliva falling from the tongue. Occasionally it would whimper and thrust its body upward in an effort to break free. The effort quickly exhausted it and the animal would slump limply again. The belly of the beast was swollen to monstrous proportions so that it resembled a hugely pregnant bitch, although Sloane could see that it was a male. The skin over the belly was stretched tight and the pink hairs bristled.

As Sloane watched, two men began to beat the dog with sticks, forcefully but obviously not at full strength. The blows were rained on the back, flanks, belly, and legs. The head was carefully avoided. Sloane called to Shin, who had stopped a few feet away from him, her face downcast, waiting for him to move on.

"Shin, what are they doing? It's cruel. Why are they doing that?"

"Not cruel. People make food."

"Then why don't they kill it and be done with it? They're *torturing* it to death."

"Not cruel," she repeated. "Give dog much rice, too much. All day push into mouth. Make dog fat. Good taste. Beat to make dog tender, good to eat. Good food for my people."

The rhythmic thumping of the sticks on the flesh was maddening to him. Shin must have sensed his thoughts. Stepping to him, she touched his sleeve.

"Come," she said. "You do not know this."

He unlaced his boots and pulled them off, leaving them outside on the matang. The floor welcomed his feet with the warmth of the earthen flues that herded hot smoke from the kitchen stove under the house before discharging it in a fanning cloud at the opposite end. Sloane marveled at the simplicity and ingenuity of the system. The heat was steady and even and made sleeping on the floor a pleasure. He never slept this well in Connecticut. Of course there was another kind of heat here, but that night they did not make love. Sloane felt feverish and nauseated. When Shin had undressed him and seen that his body did not respond, she had covered him with a quilt and watched him fall asleep. He awoke to utter blackness. He did not know where he was and started up. Her hand on his cheek stopped him and he sank back to the floor mat. It always took him a moment to piece together and gather into a whole his new life, as if it were not quite real enough to form by itself. Why, he often wondered at such a time, why can't a man simply lie where he is and not have to rush about the earth? If he could only remain there for two or three weeks, a kind of unofficial leave, a horizontal one on the simple heated floor, wouldn't a lot of things fall into place? Wouldn't he finally recuperate? Wouldn't the throbbing in his head go away?

Shin lit a kerosene lamp and in its shuddering light he saw again the dog swaying between the poles. He struggled achingly to his feet.

"Late. It's late. I don't want to, but I'd . . . better . . ."

He shook his head. She helped him dress with tenderness as though they had just made love, the warmth still within her. At the door he turned and took her crushingly in his arms for a brief moment, then he slid open the door and slipped out into the courtyard. He did not look back until he reached the road. When he did, he saw the slender pillar of wavering light where the door had not been closed all the way.

chapter twenty

The last time Sloane went to Shin his fever had abated, and so had something else. He stepped into the little kitchen garden. Within the confines of the tall bamboo fence the moonlight seemed concentrated, bleaching to pallor the grotesque gourds. It was as though they had melted in the sun and run limply into these fierce elongated shapes; then, hardened again by the cold moon, had been fixed forever, the lame and twisted hunchbacks of the garden.

He lit a cigarette and in the breathless air the smoke clung and clustered like ectoplasm.

She knows, he thought.

There was something on her face. It was more than an expression, more like the spoor of an animal. He had gazed at it while she slept, tracking the beast that eluded him there. It scampered from her mouth to her eyes, hiding beneath the lids, only to emerge and dart fleetingly across to her ears, becoming lost in the black forest above. It was a knowledge that she had and that he sought.

He heard a soft sound like the falling of a leaf and knew that it was her footstep even before he turned to see her. There was a silence about them that was difficult to break, as though the air itself had hardened into glass which encased them, making the transmission of sounds, even the movement of lips, impossible. She leaned against his arm, weightless, as though much of her had lightened into dust and blown away.

He placed his hand on the back of her neck, cupping it. His resting fingers felt the trill of her pulse, rapid and shallow, the fainting pulse of a little animal he had trapped. He had it beneath his fingertips and knew then, and without words, what she knew—that it was over, that he would not come to her again.

As he turned to leave she stood with her back to him as if she were hiding something, and Sloane remembered a story she had told him about a princess whose lover abandoned her. In the end the girl had turned into rain so that she could beat down upon him, flood him, that he might remember.

The night was graying as he walked from the village. The lark's tongue vibrated in his ear.

PART III

Brother Take

chapter twenty-one

He was awakened by a hand on his chest jostling him gently.
"Sir Doc! Sir Doc!"

Jang was calling him in a stage whisper. He had been
dreaming about his father as the mayor of a dream town, no
longer a doctor and no longer dead, or only half-dead—
once-dead—so that when Sloane Jr. asked him what to do
about the sick people lying all over the place, his father kept
saying, "That's for the authorities. This is my new assign-
ment. They've made me the mayor. I cannot do two things
at once." He wanted to keep dreaming. It was important to
find out what to do about the sick who were spilling out into
the doorways and streets of this town that was like a film set
for Dodge City or Tombstone. He opened his eyes and raised
to one elbow.

"What *is* it?"

"Boy come. Gate. Scared, Sir Doc. Brother bad sick
number ten. Pain belly. So hot. You come!"

Oh God let it not be appendicitis. He did not know how
many more anesthesialess operations he had left in him. He
could no longer bear the gagged mouths, the trembling frail
bodies wrapped round and round the table with wide adhe-
sive tape from ankles to neck, leaving a space at the
abdomen for the incision, the knuckles white and burning as

they clutched the stick thrust into their hand at the last minute by a mama-san. And the eyes—slant and roving, innocent, reproachful, enkindled with streaky frightened lights. Oh those eyes that cast out nets to drag at his arms, webs to tangle his fingers, making them heavy at the tips and ponderous. Let it be a bellyache, gastroenteritis, dysentery— something he wouldn't have to strap down, cut into.

He dressed hurriedly, pulling on but not lacing his boots. He would do that in the dispensary. When he stepped out of the tent Jang handed him a lit cigarette. As he took a long drag he saw an ambulance, headlights gleaming, idling in front of his office.

"Couldn't they bring him *here?*"

"No, Sir Doc. No can come. Too very sick. Number ten."

"It's the middle of the night." He scanned the sky. There was only an intermittent moon. "We'll be blind as roots as soon as we leave the gate. Where the fuck does he live?"

"Don't know, Sir Doc. Brother take."

Sloane forced himself to look at the boy who was to guide them. He was between nine and ten years old, small, thin, with a thick festoon of wet snot connecting one nostril to his upper lip.

"Where do you live, boy-san?"

He tried to avoid the beseechment in his eyes.

"No speak Engrish, Sir Doc. He take."

"Well wait now, Jang—how do we know how far, how long—what's the terrain—you *ask* him. We can't go flying through the night to nowhere, there's a crowd here the size of a mountain in the morning."

Jang spoke to the boy briefly.

"He shay not far, go fast."

He shay go fast my ass. Sloane climbed into the front seat of the ambulance. Jang shepherded the boy into the back behind the driver's seat. Fat Gallagher was puffing up the hill from his tent, tucking the last of his shirt into his pants. He lurched aboard and the back doors clanged to.

"Lead the way, boy-san."

Sloane had come to appreciate Gallagher for more than his deft driving. He took a certain comfort in the fact, inexplicable though it was, that Gallagher had kept gaining weight while everyone else on the post, Sloane most of all, was being shaved down to nothing. More than that, Gallagher understood that complaining constantly did not necessarily relieve the situation. When Gallagher observed an unpleasant reality it wasn't ever a gripe, it was way of recognizing the facts in order to cope with them. Such a reasonable, easygoing approach to Korea was rare among the soldiers of Sloane's acquaintance, rare enough that, however often they drove the rutted roads together, Sloane was always pleasantly surprised to see that Gallagher hadn't soured into the customary revilements.

"Where we goin, boy-san?"

Gallagher's deep Carolina mangled "boy-san" into something nearly incomprehensible, but Jang muttered to the boy and a skinny bare arm pointed up into the mountains behind the post.

"Well that narrows it," Sloane said. "Will it be safe in the dark?"

"No, sir," said Gallagher, "but we'll go up the streambed. It's dry and we'll go up far as we can, then we'll tote in, sir. Forgot my damn cigarettes."

Sloane gave him the remainder of his cigarette and sank back, defeated. The decision to go had already been made for him by the sweep of events. The ambulance moved clumsily along the road, responding to the thin voice of the Korean boy like a huge trained beast that waits for and acts on the signals of its master. Such power in that bony little body. Each time the boy spoke, Jang muttered, pointed, and the big truck veered grindingly to follow. Jang had brought cigarettes and he passed them around. In half an hour the road narrowed abruptly and dipped down into the dry bed of a stream. The stony bottom gleamed in the headlights. The gears objected, then yielded grudgingly, and they were down the incline and heading upstream. Now and then Gallagher emitted a brief yelp, whether a comment on the difficult terrain, the performance of the vehicle, or a piece of his own driving was not made clear. "Yes!" "Man!" "Ha!" *Look't that, look't that!*" "*Watch* out!" "Oh my *oh* my!" His favorite seemed to be "*That* gets it," perhaps because it could mean almost anything. Gallagher never complained, but for Sloane the pace was stupefyingly slow and the rocky bed mocked the act of sitting. So much for *go fast*. About a mile up the stream they saw a torch. It was being swung meaningfully from side to side, moving like the head of a parrot. The boy leaned out and squeaked a few phrases to which the disembodied torch responded by flouncing more giddily in the dark.

"More on, sir," Jang said with vigor. "More. More up."

The first cool wind toyed with their hair, blew their lips dry, brightened their cigarettes. It came unnoticed, skipped away and then returned a moment later, buoyed, obtrusive.

"Rain start today," Jang said to no one.

"Today?"

"Pears like now," Gallagher said, as the muted dull thrum hit the windshield, spreading to the roof. With shocking abruptness it enveloped the vehicle in a splatting wet rain that defeated the wipers. Sloane saw a second torch about fifty yards ahead, or thought he saw it, for it vanished instantly. The streambed had begun to flow. Miniature rivers bubbled up, were broken by the rocks, coalescing, casting spume, filling declivities with pools. There were shouts between Jang, the boy and the torch.

"Straight, sir," Jang said grimly. "More up."

Gallagher took a searchlight from under his seat and handed it out the window to the guide, who carried it up the stream and for another half hour they inched up the steepening incline until they saw the eyelight float morosely off to the side and ogle them in a rapid circular motion. Jang climbed out into the stream and disappeared from view, then he leaned back into the ambulance.

"Car no more. Road number ten. Stop here, Sir Doc, walk in."

If the boy's brother did in fact have a bellyache, someone was going to pay for this, dearly. And if it was something more dire, what could he do for the boy in *this?* He wanted to talk sense into someone but there was only the night itself and the night was not listening.

The litter was taken down from its rack and the four of them, each stiffening himself against the strike of the rain, plunged into the night, ankle-deep in water, unable to speak, just following the light. They had left the stream and were crossing a field of rice paddies, not bothering to seek the embankment but suck-stepping through the mud itself. It was with some astonishment that Sloane saw the light stop and when they had all joined together he saw the shadow of the farmhouse directly before them.

"Me you go in, Sir Doc," Jang said.

Sloane stepped up on the veranda and as he did so a door slid shyly open, revealing a dim flickering light. They entered and the paper door slid shut. It was like stepping into a snail shell. On a rancid pallet lay a small boy about eight years old. He wore a loose-fitting cotton shirt out of which his skinny neck stuck like a fifth extremity, topped as it was by a black thatched head, fronted by a face as creased and tightly drawn as a fist. Clusters of black flies whirred into its crevices, preening on its prominences. In their fissures the eyes roved to and fro like a pendulum counting out the minutes of his mortality. When they ran down it would be over.

Sloane knelt on the worn paper floor. The heat rose from the boy's skin in a palpable cloud. He could have warmed his hands in it. The child was even now vaporizing into angelhood. Through the oval gape of the mouth the line of dry caked teeth stood like a moldering wall. The little ribbed bellows of his chest puffed against the pressure of the swollen taut abdomen that shone in the dim light. Tight parts shine, he thought, knuckles and blisters and pus-filled belly. Sloane laid his cool palm on the boy's abdomen with a familiar reverence, reverence for the flesh he was touching and for the disease beneath it swarming in hordes, lapping into untouched corners, liquefying, caseating, necrotizing. The easiest way is to leave it encased, packaged in the body. Certainly it was neater. To cut into it, let it out, was to run the risk of having it leap up in a great wave and spread lasciviously, gleefully over the earth. The abdomen was hard, rigidly guarded, *defense musculaire* the French call it. One could have bounced a penny on it. The slight pressure of his palm produced an intense pain. The child closed his eyes hard, rocking his head, and raised a translucent hand to ward off his own. Sloane listened with the stethoscope and heard only his own pulse. A single bubble fluttered at the boy's open lips, enlarging and contracting with the shallow breaths. Outside the sound of the rain had risen. It was no longer muted and had lost its oddly musical quality. There was a roar to it, an anger, as though they were standing under a waterfall. It was louder when Sloane opened the door.

"Take him," he said to Gallagher. "Cover him with a blanket, over that a rubber tarpaulin. Cover his face. All of him."

Twists of water skirled down from the roof, forming a hanging curtain of rivulets.

"Gallagher—I don't want him jounced."

He could be so decisive and strong when it came to the patient. Sometimes it surprised him and thrilled him a little to find it in himself. It also made him question from whence that authority derived: was it from knowing what to do, or was it the illusion of knowing? He watched as the two men separated by the litter dissolved into the storm like a melting capital H. Then, turning, he bowed deeply to the family of the child. He could see their woe by the absence of emotion in their faces. These people, God damn them. Why don't they keen, wail, thrash, writhe like we would? Oh those Italians, could they suffer: falling down, sobbing, moaning with twisted clown mouths, staggering and clutching like tenors. Not Koreans. It is all drawn down into a tiny bead of pain that burns white-hot in the center somewhere, quietly and fiercely. You look at their stilled faces and you know it is there.

The mother squatted by the empty pallet, looking through the wall of the hut, her eyes seeing beyond the mud and thatch to the small mound on the stretcher pelted by rain. There were colonies of fine sweat on her nose like seed pearls. On her back and strapped to her body was an infant, his ridiculous head kicking away from hers in sleep, like a broken Kokeshi doll. The grandmother stood in the shadowy corner, staring at the floor, her tiny shoulders spilling down into a pair of gnarled hands at least two sizes too big for her. The father stood directly in front of him, holding the door, his kimchi breath coming richly through the drained face. He seemed to be listening, hearkening as it were. Sloane was relieved to thrust himself from the hut into the deluge.

They were already in the ambulance as he struggled toward the headlights, lurching, sliding, almost falling in the mud. The ambulance was now sunk halfway up the tires.

"Remember the bumps," Sloane said as he climbed into the cab. "They hurt him. A lot."

"S'all bumps all the way, sir."

"All bumps, but you have to drive *without*."

"Lucky we don't get stuck, sir. Lucky to move at all."

"The kid's got peritonitis," Sloane said. "If we don't get him back to the dispensary, he's dead. Nearly dead already, but there's a chance." A moment later he said, "Number ten chance."

"Lotta damn number tens here tonight, sir," Gallagher said.

The headlights presented a rolling wall of wetness in which no path could be discerned. In the end Sloane and Jang were out in front with searchlights, guiding the vehicle between the trees toward the streambed. Then a new sound made itself heard. At first, a murmuring like the whispering of many mouths, then louder, a slavering, a gurgling. It was a sickening sound, like that of blood spurting from a great artery. They motioned the ambulance to halt and proceeded ahead on foot. Where the stream had been they saw it rushing by, mercurial, silver, maniacal: a river. The declivity itself, acting as a natural catch basin, had collected the torrent and was racing down the mountain toward the valley. In the morning the fields would be flooded.

They might have stayed on the bank if it hadn't been for the boy. When they had climbed back into the ambulance, now on the very edge of the flood, they heard his little grunts, the *hic* at the end of each breath. And because they couldn't stand the sound of it . . . because they had invested so much in it and didn't want it all to have been for nothing . . . because the boy had paid for so many bumps already . . . but most of all because there was, in each one, as deeply placed as a soul, a private and separate reason to do it, they drove into the river. In a minute the nose of the cab was tilting into it, and in another the water was at the running board with some sliding back and forth on the floor. The ambulance took them out to the middle. It was deeper there. Sloane turned on the seat to peer into the back. Jang was hovering over the stretcher, bracing it with his body. Slone turned back in time to feel the impact of the wave like the slap of a great tail. No one spoke or cried out as the ambulance went over on its side. Sloane slid from his seat onto Gallagher, now lying heaped on the door. The vehicle was filling with water. He got himself up, pushing brutally with his boots against Gallagher's soft body and opened the passenger door. He leaped out onto the side of the ambulance and, reaching in, called out,

"The boy—pass him out quick—give him here."

Jang's brown hands appeared, holding the moaning white figure, now naked save for his long cotton shirt.

Sloane took him and retreated to the center of his small island marked by the red cross. The rain was as hard as pebbles and he buried the pallid face in his chest. The moon had slid between two masses of clouds and by its brief sickly light he could see the two men climbing up and out. They huddled together around the boy, watching as the water mischievously screened the surface upon which they stood. Then they were in it, rolling over and over, choking. Sloane saw the boy fly from his hands. He watched him rise up in the air in a kind of slow motion, his shirt ends fluttering, the wind filling out the cloth. He was no more than a torn rag. For a moment the child was hanging in the rain, his small bare arms raised, his fingers waving airily. Then by some miraculous transubstantiation he was a fish, streaking whitely across the waves, now ducking deliriously below, now gleaming in a savage curve above. Then only a twig, a piece of gray bark floating, turning lazily in the swift current, caught in a tiny serene lagoon, harbored. When they reached him he was on his back, the shining water rolling in and out of his mouth. His cracked head ribboned the stream with blood. Sloane looked back once to see the red cross emerge for a moment and then vanish for good.

All that night they walked, carrying the small body in turns. The next afternoon the father came. They gave him the body. Sloane listened while Jang told him the story of the drowning. They did not look at each other. They all kept their eyes down. When Sloane needed to clear his throat he nearly choked trying to do it soundlessly. When the father walked away with the boy it was not any different for Sloane than if he done the surgery and had failed. That was a house call, it was his house call, and there was no boy now.

chapter twenty-two

Sweetest of All Wifelets,
    This will not sound cheerful but it is meant to be.
    In this land where there is no beguiling art, no music to inspire, I have found a kind of beauty that is more exciting than all the arts. I am talking about death. But by 'death' I don't mean something morbid, I mean a dying that transcends the mere pain, strangling, and terror of it. This is rare but it exists. There is a kind of death that soars above fact. And what a lift it is to watch a man die nobly! It is truly restorative. It is too rare for one to look forward to it. And yet, in some ways, I think that I really do. Does that sound peculiar? It's absolutely true. It might sound like a warning signal, a sign of ill-health, but no, I haven't lost my buttons, not a single one. I believe it is a healthy sign for anybody posted to this place. I'll give you an example of what I mean.
    First, let me tell you that I miss you every minute. Better not send another photograph or I'll be AWOL.
    Now, here is what happened.
    Today a man was lying in a field in the shadow of his ox. The plow hung limply from the animal's neck. Six feet away and connected by a stream of blood lay the man's leg. A land mine had been struck by the blade, choosing, by some perversion of values, the man rather than the beast for its victim. We went to the edge of the field and heard his voice calling out. "What does he say?" I

asked. Jang—one of my assistants—said, "He shay no come in, Sir Doc. Too many mines here. Get killed." I said, "Ask him how badly he's bleeding." Jang said, "He shay no blood left, Sir Doc." We waited for the mine detector team and followed them in. When I reached him he was barely alive. I said, "How do you feel?" He said, "Better. Feel good now. Better." Then he took one of those deep delicate breaths and he died. But I didn't know it yet. "You're going to be all right," I said, too late by a moment.

I hope you don't go thinking that I am down in the dumps. Quite the opposite. And I hope you don't imagine I am ever going to send this. Or that I will ever be able to leave this place alive.

chapter twenty-three

Velvet evening had settled imperceptibly over Korea. Wisps of lavender smoke hung here and there above thatched roofs. There was no breeze to stir it. Above all there was no sound, as though it were a painting—russet, sere, green, fading. What gave it its life was the transmitted quivering of the rice, germinating, growing, waving in terraced fields. He could feel the life in the sodden ground bursting up, fed by the wet dust of ancestors who had eaten rice here and entered the paddies at last to give life to the next generation. It had been one of his few slow days, perhaps because a rumor of battle, of something big, had been widely circulating. To Sloane such rumors meant nothing. He tossed the butt of his cigarette and entered the dispensary.

"Anyone else?"

He stared at his hands. The fading sun made a vinelike pattern behind them on the tabletop. All day he had experienced subterranean quakes in his body. Fatigue came like the shifting of earth in his center, and when it had passed, when the matter settled into its new place, it left him lessened somehow in spirit and substance. The inability of matter to be destroyed was in the most limited sense only. Of course it could be destroyed. The empty spaces inside of him were proof.

"Onry one," Yoon said. "Mama-san, baby come more s'coshi. Pretty soon here."

Sloane sat at the table, idly making shadow pictures in the small orange beam until with sudden rudeness it was gone, taking with it the illusion of warmth. He felt unreasonably colder.

He had a revulsion for the act of childbirth that had survived his training, not lessened now by the announcement of another obstetrical case—a difficult one, he knew, since the normal ones never came to him, preferring the darkness of the huts under drifting chimney smoke, warm floors with little piles of rice straw, and an ancient mama-san to press against their grinding wombs. Only a little mound of blood and tissue on the straw, cleaned up by the kind of quiet competence seen in old arthritic hands. The complicated ones— bled out, battered, cramped to an ominous inertia in which both host and parasite lay dissipated, staring ahead at the newly realized possibility of disaster—these were the ones he saw. They took a daring, a bravado, an egotism that he no longer felt.

With effort he pushed the chair back and stood up and walked to the open door of the dispensary just as the sun sizzled out.

He saw the two figures leaving a cluster of huts and inching single-file along the narrow raised embankments that served as footpaths between the rice paddies. As they drew nearer, Sloane could see the long skirts billowing about them, a sliver of the setting sun caught in their silver hairpins, their faces expressionless, like docile beasts who register neither joy nor pain. The older woman bent upon her stick, the younger round, pausing to rest, one hand pressing the unborn child beneath her waistband. It was Shin.

Look at her, he thought as he stood outside the dispensary watching her slow climb. Thin, short of breath, using up her last strength to roll that great inappropriate belly up the hill. He did not go down the path to meet her. He waited at the top, feeling the twilight fall softly against him in suffocating purple waves. Her head was bowed and with each step she lifted her abdomen with her hands as though to roll it forward, a hiss coming through her stiffly parted lips. Ten feet away, still below him, she stopped and raised her head to include his booted feet in her field of vision.

She hates me, she must—why shouldn't she?

For a long time she stood holding herself rigidly bent, as though waiting for him to speak or walk to her. Then she made a profound bow that caused her to wobble dangerously as her center of gravity shifted. He stepped quickly forward and raised her. Her face was impervious, unreadable.

The two women followed Sloane to the treatment room, closed off partially from the rest of the Quonset hut by white plywood partitions. A homemade wooden table covered with Korean newspapers occupied the center of the room. A small table of bottles, packages, and trays stood against one wall. A tall operating lamp and a stool completed the furnishings. He gave the old woman a pile of newspapers and signaled her to help Shin undress, lie on the table, and cover herself with the paper. He walked outside and lit a cigarette.

During his first few months he had used almost exclusively Korean newspapers, having decided that these women should not be forced to deliver their babies underneath the *Stars and Stripes*. Now he could not imagine who that younger Sloane was, or how the two Sloanes were allegedly related. And yet the papers he had handed the mama-san were Korean, and that was deliberate. He shook his head over the symbolism, rather too obvious an effort—and rather too late—to be showing his respect. Perhaps he hadn't changed that much after all.

When the papers stopped rustling he reentered the room.

Shin's eyes were barely open, as though to filter the scene of all but the barest essentials. In her hands she held a smooth stick of hard wood. She would grasp it tightly with each contraction, the only outward sign of her distress. There was an embarrassed silence between them. Sloane motioned the old woman to leave.

"Where have you been?"

He hated himself for making it sound like a demand. Surely he had no rights where she was concerned.

"The house of my uncle."

"I heard nothing—" he began, but she raised one palm, arching her wrist backward, silencing him.

Later Jang told him of her ostracism, the villagers' contempt for the whore of this American officer who used to come to her at night, and of her shamelessness in the eyes of her elders. In the beginning they had thrown stones at the house and knocked down the kimchi jars in the matang and punched holes in the bamboo fence. When her pregnancy became obvious they let her alone, only spitting and cursing as they passed the house and saw her kneeling before the grinding stone. Sloane imagined her never looking up, bearing their cruelty in silence, even indifference. As her time drew near an old mama-san of the village had come to live with her, to help with the food and the chores. It was she who had come with Shin to the dispensary.

She lay on the delivery table shuddering with her contractions. There was something about her that reminded him of the dog he had seen, hanging and beaten, its swollen body stuffed with rice. It was the air of the victim. He recoiled from the thought.

The contractions were three minutes apart. Jang had told him that Shin had been in labor for twenty-four hours. She appeared weary and wan. Sloane gave her a sedative and sat down on a stool to wait. As the hours went by, Sloane noticed a lack of progress. There was no descent, no dilatation, no change save for an intermittent slowing of the fetal heart, barely perceptible. He spoke slowly and carefully to her from time to time.

Nothing to worry about . . .
You will be all right . . .
God is with you . . .
I will take care of you . . .
This is a wonderful thing . . .
You are well, the baby is well . . .
There is love all around . . .
No bad thing will ever happen to you again . . .
You will be my wife . . .
The weather will be beautiful tomorrow and forever . . .
I will never leave your side . . .

One lie after another, each one making him sadder and sorrier. She smiled faintly, whispering her thanks with the slightest exhalation.

Morning came barely noticed. He felt uplifted and frightened by her struggle. Burning white knuckles strained to break through the skin. A quiet hiss came through clenched teeth in soft bursts. A swatch of black hair escaped upon the table and through its filigree one could see the characters of the Korean newspaper spread beneath her body. Sloane stared at the newsprint as if it were a coded message from some ancient Oriental midwife who had fathomed the secrets of childbirth in this land and who had plied her trade through quiet centuries, leathery, silent, brave. If he could but read from those characters her fearless instructions, he would have it then, the way to save these two, or not even that: the way to endure it with them.

Sloane sat by her cot. His fingers slipped from the pulse at her wrist to the hollow of her palm and he clasped it tightly until the contraction was over.

Like a husband.

"Shin?"

She turned her head slowly toward him. He pointed to her abdomen, touching it with his finger, then transferred the finger to his own chest.

"Is it mine?"

He knew the answer. The question was a brutal insult but he had not meant to insult her, and yet he had to ask. She stared at him a long tine, then she nodded.

Somehow the change in the position of their hands had unlocked them from a constriction. She was talking now, rather singing out words, softly and continuously. When the pain was at its height, her voice became indefinite, slurred.

"Is the pain too bad?"

"I do not care."

"Sorry," whispered Sloane, his eyes closing in tear-blindness.

Shin's voice resumed its breathless monologue. Her *voice*, not *her*. He did not know who this pregnant woman was. And now more than ever she did not know who he was, for she included him in memories of childhood. Most of them were unfathomable, but one of them he had heard before, several times, and he could piece together how the plum blossom arrives while there is still snow on the ground. It is a surprise. In the spring garden the high rocks are covered with moss. The stone water basins look young despite their great age. She used to catch dragonflies there. Such fun. Grandfather came home to be ready for death. Didn't he remember? How grandfather was so very old and so beautiful, with his calm round face, gray hair, long beard. How beautiful his death was, quiet, peaceful, without any wrestling. His married daughters had all come home to be with him. As soon as breath had passed, uncle took a shirt of grandfather's and went up on top of the grass roof. Shook it three times. Waved farewell to the spirit. "Chuksam kache kasiow." Oh take with you this shirt. Then the wailing, low and rhythmical, mounting. *Ai-kyo. Ai-kyo. Uyi. Uyi.* Sorrow. Sorrow. Then the coffin of thick strong pine in which only pine nails are used. Pine shows the stillness of the dead, protects him from insects. High in the mountains he is carried. Neighbors. Family. Nearby is a temple of red stone with roofs like tiled boats, for the ends turn up like keels. On the way back now, listen, the tongueless bells struck by the swinging-log. How sweet the air is, hushed, ghost-colored. Grandfather! Won't grandfather be happy to see them again? And what will he think of the child! Wait until he sees . . .

For an entire day Shin had lain there with sweat and flies on her face. Sloane sat straining in wordless dialogue with that bursting womb. For hours he had known that it would end badly, that in another few hours he would see the hands relax around the clutched stick, see it fall gracelessly to the ground, see the flies crawl, dauntless now, into the nostrils beneath the rounded moons of her cheeks. He knew that normal childbirth was impossible. There were useless, feeble contractions of an exhausted womb battering against an unyielding cervix. It would be necessary to cut the cervix widely and withdraw the baby with obstetrical forceps—a pair of cupped blades to be applied separately, then hinged together at the handle. But where in rural Korea could one find obstetrical forceps, a refinement of civilized medicine? In any case the maneuver would be hazardous, the hemorrhage could prove exsanguinating. Not an obstetrician, Sloane had never performed such an operation, had only recollections of texts to guide him. OBGYN—that was Larry Olsen's specialty, and yet there were no forceps here. Olsen, home now in Jersey, contemplating his Vegas vacation.

"Jang!"

The Korean clomped across the floor in heavy boots.

"Where is the nearest provincial hospital?"

"Kaesong, Sir Doc."

"How far?"

"Eight hours, Sir Doc."

She would never survive the trip over those deeply rutted roads. He printed OBSTETRICAL FORCEPS, carefully and large, on a piece of paper, signed his name at the bottom and gave it to Jang.

"Go now. Take the Jeep, take Gallagher—go fast. When you get there, find someone who speaks English. Give him this, then bring back the package. Fast. You *cannot* rest—it has to come here *now*—number one now, understand?"

He wanted to say, "Or else this woman will die," but she could die anyway and that was not a fair burden to place on Jang.

"Make the eight hours seven," he said. "Eight is no good. Make them in six, five. No talk. Tell Gallagher to ruin the jeep if he has to. Go!"

Jang nodded, flooding his features with a smile. Sloane had learned not to return these smiles—it usually turned out to be inappropriate. It was not without a touch of envy that Sloane watched him leave, ordered from the unanesthetized core of the experience with orders to be carried out. Carried out with abandon—wildly, even. *Ruin the Jeep if he has to*—did he really say that? Where now was the public address system to which he could run and make the announcement that would bring the help he needed: *Inhalation therapy—intensive care unit—stat—inhalation therapy—intensive care unit—stat.* In the hospital the voice on the PA is nasal, uninflected. Stat: right away, now or never—emergency. But it isn't how she says it, it is what she says that makes a you-sized shadow of fear click into place in your body. Cafeteria spoons and forks pause too. Even the grave-faced painters pause over their pails, dipping brushes and wiping them more carefully. Such announcements are spells. No one who hears them is ever quite the same. Now everybody knows: on these premises lies a blue-faced gasper, a flailer, eyes bulging with the precognition of death. The skin is cold and clammy. One of us will not be going home again ever. And if that were me? And *when* that is me? He thought of the white-coated tenders bending over the struggle and rage. I have been there. I was one of them. While in the cellophane tent the dead-elect lolls, empurpled as autumn, soon to be all thumped out, fresh meat packaged in plastic. But first the ceremony: needles in the arms and the legs, the heart even, the body draped with cords and tubes. Beep-beep-beep in a prayer for the dying. But that was not Shin. Shin was an earth-filled bottle into which he had dropped a seed. The grown plant had filled the bottle with roots and convolutions and needed release in order to live in the air and the rain.

文

A sudden jerk of his head informed Sloane that he had been dozing, or nearly.

Midday held its breath, unwilling to relieve the humid pressure with a single exhalation.

A day had passed, a day of whispers, rustle, panic. The heartbeat slowed, was barely perceptible beneath the protuberance of the abdomen. The newspaper was marked with red in an ever-increasing stain. Shin's eyes roved slowly in the blindness of exhaustion and pain. Occasionally they met his, fastened for an instant and moved on.

Outside the old woman waited.

When Jang returned he was dusty and sweaty and looked as if he hadn't slept for a week. When he passed Sloane the shapeless parcel and stepped away, he nearly fell backwards. Sloane unwrapped it swiftly and held it to the light. In his hand was a single shining metal instrument, one blade of a pair of obstetrical forceps. One useless blade. MADE IN GERMANY. The difference between an instrument and a weapon: another blade. Sloane had an impulse to laugh, then he wanted to strike out against Jang, who smiled now in expected approbation. As quickly as the questions came flooding into his brain—Didn't you check to *see?* What moron *gave* this to you? What kind of a fucked up country *is* this?—he saw that it was really his fault, for he had violated the very first rule he had learned, or thought that he had learned in Korea: you're in the United States Army but this is not America, don't ever forget it, and don't take anything for granted.

He laid it carefully aside, *the forcep*, like a piece of fragile glass that might be scratched by the slightest trauma. He turned toward Shin. He cut deeply into the womb neck. Her warm blood cascaded over his hands and hung in rivulets from his elbows, then ran into his armpits and down his sides. Reaching into the torrent Sloane felt a foot. He pulled. There were knees. Thighs. Buttocks. Cord. Shoulders. Arms. Head. Blood. A gurgling sound. A cry. A life. He placed the infant on the girl's breast and watched the stick slip from her pale hand to the floor with the faintest of clatters.

When they took her back to the village, the chief looked at the girl briefly, then he looked out and away toward the hills.

"Jang," Sloane said. "Tell him to bury her with her uncle."

After a brief exchange, the chief nodded, then he said something to Jang in another tone. The shift was slight but Sloane had perceived it. He couldn't decipher it but he knew that it was not meant for him. On the way back to the base he asked Jang what was said.

"Just 'Okay,' Sir Doc. Everything okay."

"No," Sloane said. "After that he said something else. What did he say?"

"No, Sir Doc, shay fine okay, go with uncle okay okay, Sir Doc."

"You're a good man, Jang," Sloane said, "but this is number ten lie. Now tell me the truth."

Jang looked as if he wanted to leap out of the vehicle. He looked down into his lap a long time.

"Chief shay: 'Always, soldier all around to kill good girl like Shin.'"

PART IV

Beyond the Yalu River

chapter twenty-four

He kept the baby for six weeks. It wasn't hard. During the
day it was at the dispensary, at night in Sloane's tent. In face,
hair, color—in every way it was Korean. Sloane lay on his
cot and listened. The sound it made was not unlike mice
scuffling in a cage, or small twigs brushing against a house.
During the day it would have gone unheard, but at night—
what a din. In the dim light he could see the high sides of the
basket jiggling. A thump brought him wearily to his feet to
peer through the netting. He flicked on his flashlight and,
shielding its direct rays, examined the turmoil within. Two
glistening black beads, two fists punching wildly at the air.

He had kept newborn babies in his tent before. Once it
had been twins. Sloane recalled the mother nosing her belly
from side to side like a cow or a merchant ship in which the
cargo shifts unexpectedly in the hold. He had thought at
once that there might be twins. She had been one of his first
deliveries. It was done on the floor with the woman fully
clothed and on all fours, knees apart, straining. All his efforts
to impose a more Western posture on this experience failed.
In the end he yielded to the local culture, save for the most
difficult cases. He had reached up beneath her long skirt and,
drenched in amniotic fluid, caught the infant blindly. When
she did not rise or lie down after the first baby came but

remained on all fours, straining still, he had felt the full belly and waited for the second. There was excitement and suspense in the dispensary then. Many came to see the twins: American soldiers in heavy boots tiptoeing for the first time in years; Korean soldiers, their faces stony, untranslatable; officers with English-looking swagger sticks, finding in these babies a tiny reminiscence of some far-off private softness. Gallagher had said, "This is some kinda Christmas."

He remembered first holding up the babies for the mother to see. He remembered how she sucked in her breath and looked away. Her husband had not come. The principle of defilement had kept him away. It was a taboo, and curiously Sloane felt himself sharing man's aversion for—or was it a fear of?—childbirth. It seemed wisdom to turn aside from such an exclusively female world. But how had it evolved? Was it avoidance of guilt? Did it have to do with fear of replacement by the son? Or, more simply, with the preservation of sex? He thought of his own role in these deliveries as quasi-legitimate, a violation of the taboo. He should not be there, it was forbidden, not to be looked upon by man. Yet, he thought, a woman cannot approach the delivery of a child with the same spirituality as he could. It was his maleness that shuddered, half in reverence, half in marvel, feeling the mysticism, the uniqueness, the terror, revulsion, and joy of childbirth. No, a woman could feel sympathy or share the remembrance of pain endured, but a woman could not marvel the way a man could.

There was a room in the dispensary where the woman who had delivered remained overnight. For the usual case twenty-four hours was sufficient to observe them for complications and to administer whatever medications might be needed. He had kept the twins a few days longer. He remembered watching the infants swaddled and strapped to the backs of two women who had come to take them home and assist the mother. They were smiling as they left, bowing. The next day he had ordered his bag packed and with Jang left the post to see the infants and their mother in the village. An old man carried his long pipe into a field to examine the new rice shoots. A red ox stared stupidly from its tether. There was the smell of kimchi putrefying in the courtyard crocks. Nothing new, nothing different. He entered the matang, cluttered with objects of farmlife: the mat covered with red peppers drying in the sun, the round stone-on-stone used for grinding, the chickens rocketing across the yard. And there, on the narrow ledge just outside the sliding doors, he saw two bundles of cloth.

He had walked straight to them, opened the bundles one by one, and saw the little gray faces. Saw the dent in one tiny head, saw the narrow necks twisted and limp. He placed them back on the ledge, the head of one upon the other's chest, light and shadow dappling their skin, cold as dolls. Then he had stepped on the ledge and slid open the door. On the floor mat she lay, eyes closed, mouth slightly open, the light sparking the gold in her teeth. At the sound of the door she turned and looked at him with the same stupid stare as the tethered ox. With recognition, a smile of utmost shyness appeared on her face.

"Why?"

Sloane wanted Jang to ask her but Jang shrugged.

"Dunno, Sir Doc, too poor people here. No can feed."

"*Ask* her," Sloane ordered coldly.

Jang hesitated.

"*Ask* her, I said, *damnit* Jang do *one thing I ask you.*"

He was recklessly angry. In a dream he would have killed them all.

Jang and the woman conversed in Korean for a long time.

"What? What does she say? How long do I have to wait? Do I have to place her under arrest? Give me an answer goddamnit."

Jang looked from Sloane to the woman and back to Sloane again. He looked as if he wondered whether Sloane would attack her.

"Shay . . . two baby rike dog, rike cat. Not nice. Too bad ruck."

Of course if he had known he would never have given them up. As to how you manage that—"You can't take your children home because you're going to kill them"—he did not have a clue. Nor could he imagine how he might have asked the question that had haunted him ever since: "Why didn't you kill just one?"

He was bringing his child to the orphanage at Seoul and he was going to visit the Carmelite convent on the way. He had heard that the Carmelites were living in poverty in their cloister with a great need for rice and cloth for their habits. He had sent to Tokyo for bolts of wool and, upon their arrival, together with two one-hundred pound sacks of rice and the infant in a basket, he had set out with Jang and a Korean driver on the road to Seoul. He held the basket on his lap to protect the infant from the jarring and from time to time he examined it clinically. On entering the city, the big ambulance creaked along the narrow crowded streets. Seoul was a huge simmering pot of stew, rich and rotten, into which had been thrown naked children, white-pantalooned sad-faced women, thin bony men, flies, kimchi, dried fish and sewage. The afternoon sun was oppressive as they turned the labyrinthine streets.

They came upon the convent after many false turns. The ambulance lurched to a halt and Jang nodded vigorously, smiling, despite the absence of signs on the doorpost. The three men left the ambulance, Sloane with the baby cradled in his arms leading the way. The convent sat among a swirl of trees and vines, the only green since passing the city gates. Through the foliage they could see the face of the convent, aged, silent. They approached the entrance and waited, certain that their presence had been noticed.

A nun appeared from around the side of the yellowish earthen building. She was a so-called working nun, one of the few not purely contemplative. He studied her large lumpish form beneath its brown habit. Her face was an impassive bronze with high Korean cheekbones. A slight bow and Jang told her that Sloane was a lieutenant come with rice and new cloth for their habits. She bowed and led them to a small shaded area of the garden in back. The strawberries were ripe on the vines. A single red cow appeared from behind a bush. Sloane clumped after the nun, his boots slamming the wooden floor, raising echoes.

The room he entered was small, square, and barren, save for a rattan chair and a small table. He sat in the chair facing the only object in the room that demanded any attention, a large wooden grille comprising a portion of one wall. Beyond the grille was darkened space.

The minutes were extraordinarily empty, punctuated by the exaggerated sounds of flies, an intermittent creaking of the rattan, and once a shocking scrape of the chair leg as he shifted position. A green celadon bowl filled with strawberries stood on the table. He took one and it bit him sharply on the lips.

He sat for half an hour as the heat and the silence did their subtle work. The tiniest fragment of his consciousness surrendered to the languor and he dozed. The speck of him that remained waited before the grille as the audience in a theater waits in the dark for the curtain to rise. At one point he thought that he was bringing the baby to Kate, showing her the prize he had won in the war. He was somehow aware of a dim flowing of black shapes behind the grille and he awoke to the stirring of the infant on his lap. He placed the baby in its basket of woven rattan on the floor beside the chair. A gauze curtain was drawn aside and behind the grille he saw three black-robed, black-cowled nuns.

They were seated facing him. The afternoon sun streamed through the carven lattice of the grille. The nuns wore black veils across the lower half of the face, concealing all but the eyes and a small patch of forehead. The nun in the center spoke first in a deep, old-woman's French, pure even in its quaver.

"You are welcome to Carmel. I am Mother Beatrix, the Superior here. I wish to thank you for the gifts of cloth. And for the rice. They will be used."

He gave polite assurance. The nuns who had been seated motionless moved now. The total absence of angles in their outline caused it to appear that they were, in fact, physically united. They bent forward together and the effect was that of wind passing over a rice paddy.

They had seen the child. Did they know that it was his?

Sloane wondered how it was that these Carmelites, a cloistered group of nuns, contemplative in purpose—nuns who had taken the vow of silence—were speaking to him now.

The dark shapes were still, their spectral hands clasped in their laps like three sleeping doves. Now and then a white bird would slowly unfold, take wing, rise gently into the air and float across the grille in a small arcuate flight, to fall again into its shadow lap-nest. It had sought nothing, had flown nowhere, yet seemed fulfilled. They bent again as though a wind bore their gauze forward and he held the basket up that they might see the child with less effort. The elderly nun spoke again with deep vibrato.

"And the child?"

In halting French he told the story. Then he said, "I have kept him until now to ensure his survival. I am bringing the baby to the orphanage of Tong Dong Po. The Sisters of St. Paul have agreed to take him." Then he added, "This is the most that I can do." Still uneasy, he said, "I have been told St. Paul's will be a safe place for him . . . and he will receive an education there. It is apparently a very good place to take a child . . . such as this." There was no response, only a nod—and yet he did not feel judged, not by them. Who, then, was judging him?

He asked about the life of the convent.

"Ah," the old nun said. "Life in Carmel is *très gai*," and she smiled as though recalling moments of naughtiness. "We are silent, you know, save for our prayers, and on rare occasions, such as your most honored and generous visit. But we much enjoy each other's company. We speak with our eyes and hands and often merely with our thoughts. In this way, what marvelous fun we share."

"But how do you live?"

"We pray. That sustains us."

"Do you not ever long to have a family?"

She smiled.

"We are a family, a joyous one. And we have the Holy Family with us all the time. But you know that. This is true for any convent."

"What do you eat?"

"What do we eat? Often the poor will bring us gifts, and we have a garden. Did you taste our strawberries?"

Her head tilted coquettishly in a single small gesture that bespoke her gardener's pride, and with the faintest touch of mischief she left the next moment vacant. He filled it with the anticipated praise. The nuns bent together with obvious pleasure. He pressed further.

"Do you never go hungry?"

"Never. Our hunger is not for food."

"For what, then?"

"Grace."

The word was loosed from her with the softness of a silken sash dropping to the floor. He remembered the small splash of a tern as it cast itself into the quiet morning sea.

"How long have you lived here?"

"Twenty years ago four of us came from France to build this convent. Of these four, two are left, and we are now twenty-eight. The others are Korean."

"Have you never left these confines?"

"Never."

"But . . . the world is beautiful and . . . lively. "

There was a pause.

"Do you find the war lively, Lieutenant Sloane?"

With that question alone she redefined the meaning of *cloistered* for him, for she said it with an innocence layered with as sharp an understanding of the world as he had heard anywhere in Korea.

Sloane shifted uncomfortably. His gaze fell upon the sleeping baby beside him on the floor. He felt a sudden surge of attachment to the child. The baby stirred, stretched one arm and slept again. Certainly, back to Kate and the commons at Yale, the dinner parties, the Yale functions at restricted country clubs, that would all work out, Kate would love them both and he would have a Korean son who would follow in his footsteps.

"There is a young nun here who has made a great sacrifice," the nun said softly. "Before Sister Han Ae came to Carmel she was a singer. It was said that she had the most beautiful voice in all Korea. Of course at any one time there are many with the finest of voices in Korea." She smiled at this. "She chose to enter Carmel and renounce her singing forever. Now she sings only for us during our chanting. Her voice *is* beautiful. Surely the gifts of the world would have been hers. We know the depth of her sacrifice."

Sloane realized that this was another answer to his question about leaving the world behind.

"May I hear her?"

The Mother Superior seemed lost in thought.

"You have come, a rare visitor to us. Your kindness is great and your baby is beautiful."

She nodded her assent.

The subtlest of rustles attended the nun's appearance behind the screen as she joined the others. She made no sign of acknowledgment of the stranger's presence. Yet in the spike of her stance and in the points of pink upon each thrusting cheek there was a mute recognition of her role. Sloane felt a little drunk looking at her, to a degree that he did not trust himself. Unveiled, her face was a lonely beam-less moon, afloat in the black sky, without fire, without ice.

With a small upturn of the chin she began to sing.

He was unprepared for this, a silver soaring soprano. *Ave Maria*, the voice rich and reverent, rising and falling in fragile significance. She sang with intelligence and ardor. *Ora pro nobis*. The notes formed like beaded silver on her lips and fell into the air reluctant to be borne from her, spilling to fruition on his ears.

When she finished, the silence stunned him. What he heard next was the unruly bawling of the child.

chapter twenty-five

Sloane had known that the front was shifting, had heard
even that the line had buckled under a new series of Chinese
charges. He knew it intellectually, that is, but felt no terror
at the reports that came to his desk with increasing fre-
quency on the need to rehearse emergency mobilization and
evacuation from the medical facility. After all, he reasoned,
it is supposed to have an ebb and flow, and he felt somehow
magically encircled, insulated from it. He was a doctor doing
his duty. That the action was drawing closer was evident
from the distant sound of the big guns, which could be heard
constantly now. At the first barrage he had paused and
looked off across the valley with the others. No time to grow
thoughtful. They're our guns, so get on with it.

When the battle came, it was with the suddenness of an
epileptic seizure. He had always had a childhood idea of battle: shouts and the beating of hooves . . . chain-mail and
lances quilling above snorting war beasts . . . stripes of bow-
men with their weapons poised on rigid arms while inside
giddy princes gloated in vertigo. At the end there would be
stains of red upon the caparisons and men leaning from their
horses, their delicate beards pointing at the sky in the
moment of death. What came now was cold, metallic, mal-
odorous, painful.

Running, he saw over his shoulder the dispensary burst into a momentary chrysanthemum, then only a black hole full of swirling fumes. There was no chance to lead or to list, or any of the other items on the sheet of Standard Operating Procedures. Sloane ran, following Jang and Yoon and the rest. They hid in the paddies, staring at the night sky. In an hour the firefight was over. Yoon's face ran red for the second time, and Sloane, gazing down at the dead boy, had a terrible moment of déjà-vu. Jang rocked back and forth, wailing in a reed-like voice that did not sound human. When the machine-guns started up again, Jang led Sloane away. Now Sloane would obey Jang's slightest command, their roles entirely reversed. When Jang said "Run, Sir Doc!" he ran, "Here, Sir Doc!" he followed. In moments of rest, Sloane could not avoid musing on this easy disappearance of rank and order. In defeat, in retreat, he was Jang's soldier, listening eagerly for the next order, confident in his leader's benevolence and wisdom.

Seven days later, the two reached Seoul.

The Chinese had come crashing into the city. It was a blister, swollen to the bursting point with fires and the crumbling detritus of war. Sloane found himself with Jang in the lacerated city attempting to avoid the firefights that erupted around them at each intersection. They scuttled in a crouch from building to wall, from a fiery alley to a street ulcerated by bomb craters. There was the incessant rataplan of small-arms fire beating in no rhythm, assailing with cold surprise. Gray men cringed and scurried by them in the acrid air, some with guns pointing from their middles, fingering the night with frightened accusation. Others lay upon the fuming stones with great smeared clots on them, staring. Sloane could not tell living from dead, friend from foe. The noise of battle became less brisk as they ran, and Sloane guessed that they had crossed a line of fire into a quieter place that the storm had just swept. It had the look of antiquity, as though these ruins had stood for a thousand years.

A commotion at the end of the street caught Sloane's ear, and stealthily he and Jang sidled to a vantage point. They recognized the yellow building as the Carmelite convent. There were great blasted holes in its walls through which he saw the nuns standing in the ruins of the cloister. Soldiers were there, pushing them toward the door, jabbing with their guns. The two French nuns were in the vanguard followed by a score of their Korean sisters. Then they were outside, walking in the street, welcomed back into the world with a shrill curse, punched and pushed along the alien ground they had sacrificed twenty years before. When Sloane stood to follow their progress with his gaze, a shot rang out and a spray of stones struck his back. Standing upright and presenting himself in full view, he raised his hands in surrender and walked toward the nuns. Jang did the same.

For months they were marched northward toward the Yalu River on the border of Manchuria. Nuns, soldiers, missionaries, consular officials, and White Russians. It was incomprehensible to Sloane why an army of any nation would need, or want, to march this disparate group from any one place to another. Neither alone nor together did they constitute a threat of any kind. Few of the soldiers were fit for fighting. Wherever they were headed, what would the army do with them there?

For the first few days of the march he had been unable to turn his gaze from the nuns. From a distance, they looked like awkward storks pointing their white cornets in precise staccato rhythms as they rocked and bent along the road. The weeks had passed and the cornets were no longer white. Those that remained sagged, gray and dirty, about their heads. The others had fallen to the ground like sick birds.

The wearer would flinch imperceptibly, half-turn as though to reach for it, then, without stopping, plod on, pulled by the automatic rhythm of captivity.

They had come to a place called Mal-Tong. It had the ring of a curse. The town lay bellying the ground like a dead beetle, lifeless, smokeless, without response to the rays of the westering sun that played across it back and forth, probing for some sign of life. They had been herded into a street, the ends of which were quickly sealed off by guards. The torpid summer day had drained their strength. A sudden breeze appeared and he submitted gracefully to it. The wind licked his skin and, opening his eyes, he let it brush across the hot globes. When the rain came, at first a spray, quickly a stinging torrent, he was alive to it. Once or twice he had wept in the rain. It was a good concealment. The ground turned from dust to mud with startling swiftness. There were slight slidings and sinkings here and there in the lines of prisoners as they settled softly in the mud. The order came to move on.

The throng shuddered and inched slowly down the street, not so much walking as slithering, a long worm whose segments did not fit together. His progress was interrupted by an abrupt collision with Sister Han Ae, who had not moved with the rest. He watched her struggling to raise one foot from the mud. One knee lifting in a long skirt, she leaned far to the left in an effort to extricate her right leg. With a sucking noise that seemed indecorously loud, her foot came free minus the shoe that had encased it. She looked vacantly at her bare foot for a moment and moved on, limping in the mud. Sloane moved quickly to the spot, bent, and scooping away mud with his hands, dug out the black-laced oxford and hurried to her side. He handed her the shoe and they walked silently together toward the abandoned Japanese jail where they were to be housed while they were in Mal-Tong.

Mal-Tong was one of an endless succession of jails, empty at their arrival and sorrowfully silent when filled with prisoners. They trudged in lines into the large bare rooms and lowered themselves to the boards. The ability to make noise had slipped away from them. They had become substanceless, specters that floated to rest on the floor. Sloane and Jang often exchanged glances but they seldom spoke a word. The only sound was the staccato barking of a North Korean guard and the occasional crack of a blow rippling off into a half-dozen sobs.

chapter twenty-six

My Dear Kate,

How does one know when he has come to the outer reaches of his mind? That is to say, used up his brain, extruded it like paste through the molded chinks of his skull, to be left an empty husk, an old coconut from which the last thin milk has been sun-sucked?

It's shamefully easy to write this, as I am writing it in my head, this old dry head. I may have to stop in the middle of a sentence, a word even, if the fluid runs out or if they catch me, the guards, tinkering, scribbling, mumbling like this, as if you could hear this drivel across 10,000 miles.

Let's see what I have. Is there anything? I believe I have one thing left: I am afraid to be beaten or killed.

That. They haven't been able to take that away.

I love it, my fear. It keeps me eating the slops, lifting my legs in the act of walking, sleeping, squatting by the side of the road. I have this awful fear of being beaten to death like the others and leaving my flesh in the wilderness.

Why am I writing this way?

Don't even ask. I don't care any more what you think or what I say. It doesn't matter. I do not know whether I have the strength to live again on your terms, to care again whether I own a Chevrolet or a Ford, a G.E. or a Frigidaire, or whether I play tennis or golf or whether I work, fight, drink. I know death and I *know disease. And I know about the absence of miracles. About that you can ask me anything. For now I will tell you it is horrible to live without them, even worse to hope for them as shamelessly as I have.*

My feelings have become rather primitive
I don't understand love the way I did.
Now I shall love the one who feeds me.

If I am a dog now, I shall be the best dog that a long-ago surgeon out of Yale could ever be. And I will tell you something else. It's about this collar around my neck. I could feel it forming from the moment I entered Korea. This war, this country, had designs on me. It was to put me in this condition. In fact the whole thing started even before that. It is now my belief that in the envelope directing me to Fort Sam Houston was the invitation to wear this collar and be a dog, a good little dog, a Yankee dog for the sake of some sadistic enterprise. I couldn't have known it then. Now I know the secret. When something, whatever it is, arrives in the mail, don't open it. That's a small price to pay for your freedom, your dignity, your life—no mail. If you do open the mail and someone in the army tells you to go somewhere, don't do it. Go the other way.

chapter twenty-seven

Sloane remembered the first beating he had witnessed early in the march. With it he had experienced the electricity of hate. He had seen the boot grinding into the neck of an American soldier, crushing the trachea with its weight, saw the blackening face of the youth and the struggle, at first for self-control in the knowledge that resistance would provoke a fatal blow, then the moment when the soldier understood that the boot on his neck was the end. With that realization came the desperate quivering of the body, the flailing of the arms, the bulging sidestare of the eyes. Beyond pain, knees drawn up, head raised and rocking on his back like a stiff doll, a few convulsive moments, then a falling away, a loosening, a settling into lifelessness.

That was long ago. Now they watched like antelope in the tall grass. Restraint, which came ill-dressed and clumsy at first, yielded to passivity. Only the fear that tomorrow the tiger must feed again moved in their dull and secret minds.

Tonight Sloane and Jang squatted near Sister Han Ae. At one end of the room the guards were ladling warm cabbage water into bowls. As the bowls were passed hand to hand, they sat leaning against a wall to face the crowd. In the midst of the prisoners, a thin arm reached up from the floor, holding a bowl toward the guard who walked among them. Sloane saw the guard kick away the arm, sending the wooden bowl clattering to the floor. There followed the rapid report of Korean rasped from an outraged throat.

"More? You ask for *more?*"

Then the thud of boots again and a faint underflowing chorus of sighs. Sloane was close enough to see the guard's face. As the beating progressed it seemed to him that the cruelty fed upon itself, taking strength from its own excess, rising in crescendo. Initially it seemed a monotonous beating, but something about the man's face let him know that this time the guard might not be able to temper his hatred, might rollick past the point of salvage and deliver that final blow. Jang felt it too. Sloane saw him sitting at first, then rising and squatting as if swelling to an action.

With a suddenness that took Sloane by surprise, Jang stood, still staring at the soldier. There was a moment's pause, a hanging between stillness and motion, and he bent toward the beating. Sloane reached out his hand now, encircling one of Jang's thin ankles, and stopped him.

"Jang. Please."

Jang paused and looked down at him. He seemed smaller now, with round shoulders that fairly cascaded from his neck, giving the soft muted outline of a figure drawn in charcoal. The skin was stretched tautly across his face reflecting the dim light from his brow and cheeks. Sloane saw the dry teeth hung between Jang's furious lips, the vigor of his stare from which all elements of resignation had gone and which brimmed with a liquid that could have been the ichor of madness or hate. He roughly kicked away the restraining hand and ran toward the beaten soldier.

"Jang!"

The guard did not see him approaching from the rear, and became aware only when Jang had flung himself upon him, tearing at his face with his fingers, pulling his cheeks, nose, and lips into rubbery contortions. The guard whirled and tore at his arms. They closed upon each other now in a locking union that swayed and tilted above the dying soldier. Jang was grappling at the throat of the guard now and, stunned by his strength, the guard seemed unable to tear away. He was groping for the gun at his belt when a shot rang across the room, a single crack that sent Jang spinning into a half-circle. With an unearthly deliberateness of motion he looked down at the ground and settled almost languorously upon the soldier's body. The guard's breath came in a kind of sucking sob as he emptied his pistol into the two bodies, the bullets passing first through Jang, then the soldier. The shots sent a monotonous echo across the room. It quavered over the heads of the prisoners bending to sip from their bowls.

文

Who was this man called Jang, whose name was like hot metal, with a square small head, rowdy, afraid of the dark, and behind whose bright eyes ghosts and spirits pranced and waved?

"What did you do before?"

"Before, sir?"

"Before . . . *this*."

"Ah, before. Cibilian. Jang father bellmaker, mace bell. Big iron bell for temple and door. Hot, hot, pound with hammer makee nice bell shape. Then carve message. Pretty soon takee market, sell'm good."

One very bad night during Sloane's slow recovery from malaria, Sloane had reached out with an arm as heavy as though it were dipped in slow-running oil and let it spill onto the Korean's arm. His numb fingers seemed turgid and swollen so that he barely felt the smoothness and warmth of the yellow-brown skin. What did come through was the hardness of the flesh. Was it all those bells in his past that had sent layers of iron settling into his body? Into his spirit, too, piling like crusts around his core. To Sloane he was as pure, as hard, as distant as one of those tongueless Korean bells, hung in a temple, struck to response by the slightest tapping. Jang was the sound of those bells transubstantiated into flesh. And he was loyal as a bell, too, that never failed to answer.

That night Sloane devoted his small portion of energy, before falling asleep, to devising a way of taking his own life. There was no debate, nor even any thought—he was too tired for that and too decisive. The goal was not to get himself killed—that would not do. No, he would commit the deed himself. Exactly how he didn't know yet. It would have to be sure-fired. He mustn't be rash about it. If it took another week, that would be endurable. From the plan itself he would take fortitude. Then he would prove that he was not really a dog. And then he would feed the earth on which his son would thrive.

chapter twenty-eight

One day the prisoners found themselves abandoned with the guns and other booty. It was a long ride south to Seoul. Sloane tried to recognize the silhouette of a hill against the sky, a clump of trees, a rock formation. Nothing. It was terra incognita. The march had faded not only from his life but from the land itself.

He spent a week in a military hospital in Seoul. He did not write to Kate. In that direction he was, for the moment, speechless. Once he asked about the orphanage of the Sisters of St. Paul. No one seemed to know and he did not ask again. As for what it meant that he was leaving his son behind in Korea, he assumed he would be asking that question for the rest of his life. Now all he knew was that it wasn't in his orders, wasn't in the books or the lectures by Uncle Sam, wasn't in the stars that he saw—or would have seen had it not been raining—on his honeymoon with Kate.

Sloane returned to what remained of his unit to wait for the call to embark on the plane. It took three days. He never left the barracks excepting a drink in the officers' club. He told no one his story. It was the story of a prisoner, not comparable to the stories of battle with which the officers were buzzing over their whiskey. One evening he thought he saw Gallagher and called out to him but the boy did not answer. He looked a little thinner but of course it was Gallagher. Sloane called out again, then he stepped in front of the boy. They shook hands warmly but conversation was impossible.

"Lost my hearing, Doc," Gallagher said. "Sorry I can't hear you."

Sloane wanted to ask whether the loss was permanent and he thought of writing the question down on his pad, but the thought frightened him, perhaps because it was too close to doctoring, and doctoring again in Korea— doing anything but leaving it—was not to be admitted into consciousness.

"See they got you down to the bone, sir," Gallagher said. "But *man* it's good to see you alive, sir."

Gallagher must have known or guessed that Sloane was rotating out, for when they shook hands again he said, "Proud to know you, sir. I remember them two twins. *That* was a time."

When at last the plane shuddered, roared in pain and thrust itself from the disgusted earth, Sloane leaned against the window and watched as the peaks and valleys barreled away, diminishing like a planet. Shin. Jang. Yoon. His son without a name. How much loss was he bringing back with him? A few of his patients had had leprosy, their sores oozing into his ungloved hands. He had long since gotten over the shock, but it was hard not to wonder whether one day he would approach the mirror, expecting to lather his face, and there would be Korea in the form of leprosy. But then, wouldn't he see it, Korea, in his face anyway? Wouldn't he hold it in his hand every time he moved the scalpel? At the Yale-New Haven Hospital his colleagues had moved up the ladder, familiarizing themselves with the latest technology— but what did they know of a surgical forcep?

The best way to enter a country like this is by shipwreck, he thought. Tossed and skimming between glossy green peaks, frozen with dread, to flotsam clung, then flipped onto sharp rocks—it doesn't matter—saved. Then there could be no regret, no cynicism, only an awareness that things might have been worse. Then everything that came later would be added on to life. There would be, by definition, no possibility for subtraction.